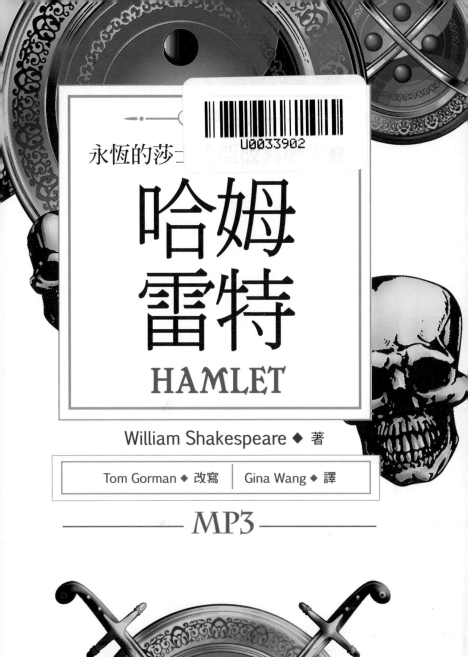

永恆的莎士比亞

哈姆雷特

HAMLET

William Shakespeare ◆ 著

Tom Gorman ◆ 改寫 | Gina Wang ◆ 譯

— MP3 —

永恆的莎士比亞改寫劇本 ❶

哈姆雷特
Hamlet

作　　者	William Shakespeare, Tom Gorman
翻　　譯	Gina Wang
編　　輯	Gina Wang
校　　對	黃詩韻
內文排版	陳瀅竹
封面設計	林書玉
製程管理	洪巧玲
出 版 者	寂天文化事業股份有限公司
電　　話	+886-(0)2-2365-9739
傳　　真	+886-(0)2-2365-9835
網　　址	www.icosmos.com.tw
讀者服務	onlineservice@icosmos.com.tw
出版日期	2016 年 7 月 初版一刷

版權所有 請勿翻印
郵撥帳號 1998620-0 寂天文化事業股份有限公司
劃撥金額 600（含）元以上者，郵資免費。
訂購金額 600 元以下者，加收 65 元運費。
〔若有破損，請寄回更換，謝謝〕

國家圖書館出版品預行編目 (CIP) 資料

永恆的莎士比亞改寫劇本：哈姆雷特 / William Shakespeare, Tom Gorman 作；Gina Wang 譯 . -- 初版 . -- 臺北市：寂天文化 , 2016.07
　面；　公分
ISBN 978-986-318-469-0 (平裝附光碟片)

873.43357　　　　　　　　　　　105010409

Contents

Introduction 🎧

About 500 years ago, Hamlet's father, the king of Denmark, was murdered by his own brother, Claudius. Then Claudius quickly married Hamlet's mother, Gertrude. As the play opens, Hamlet's father's ghost appears and tells his son who murdered him. He urges Hamlet to seek revenge. As the play unfolds, Hamlet tries to convince himself that he should murder Claudius.

This is Shakespeare's most famous play, known for the anguished character of Hamlet.

Cast of Characters ⌒₂

HAMLET, PRINCE OF DENMARK: Son of the dead King Hamlet, and nephew of the present King of Denmark

CLAUDIUS, PRINCE OF DENMARK: Hamlet's uncle

GERTRUDE: Queen of Denmark and Hamlet's mother

GHOST: The ghost of Hamlet's murdered father

POLONIUS: Chief adviser to Claudius

HORATIO: A commoner and loyal friend of Hamlet

LAERTES: Son of Polonius and the brother of Ophelia

OPHELIA: Daughter of Polonius and the sister of Laertes

ROSENCRANTZ AND GUILDENSTERN: Former classmates of Hamlet

VOLTIMAND AND CORNELIUS: Danish courtiers

MARCELLUS, BERNARDO, AND FRANCISCO: Guards at the castle

REYNALDO: Polonius's servant

OSRIC: A Danish courtier

GRAVEDIGGERS, LORDS, ATTENDANTS, ACTORS, AND SERVANTS

ACT 1

Summary

赫瑞修和守衛們決定告知哈姆雷特關於其亡父鬼魂出現在艾辛諾爾城堡外一事，同時，葛簇特和克勞地希望哈姆雷特停止再為其父之死而哀悼。當他們離開該處，哈姆雷特吐露他的想法，若非神的律法，他早因悲慟父親之死和母親之恥而自戕。其母在丈夫去世不到兩個月的時間，下嫁遠不如父王的克勞地，此舉令哈姆雷特感到震驚。

當哈姆雷特聽聞父親的鬼魂出現，他決定與其對話，並要求他人保密。雷爾提在前往巴黎前，要歐菲莉亞小心哈姆雷特對她的追求，以保衛她的貞操與聲譽。波隆尼爾接著給予雷爾提行為上的建議，並要歐菲莉亞避免與哈姆雷特共處，她也答應這麼做。

午夜時分，先王的鬼魂告訴哈姆雷特王子，他被克勞地謀殺，哈姆雷特承諾要替父王報仇。

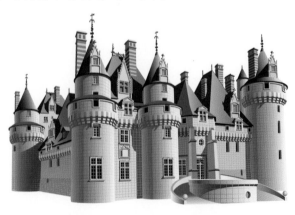

Scene 1

(**Francisco** is at his post before the castle in Elsinore.
Bernardo enters.)

BERNARDO: The clock has struck 12.
I'll take over the watch now, Francisco.

FRANCISCO: Thank you for relieving me.
It is bitter cold, and I am sick at heart.

BERNARDO: Has it been quiet tonight?

FRANCISCO: Not a mouse stirring.

BERNARDO: Well, good night. Tell my
Partners on watch to hurry.

FRANCISCO: I think I hear them now.

(**Horatio** and **Marcellus** enter as **Francisco** exits.)

MARCELLUS: Hello, Bernardo!

BERNARDO: Welcome, Horatio and Marcellus.

MARCELLUS: Has it appeared again—the *thing*?

BERNARDO: I have seen nothing.

MARCELLUS: Horatio says it is only our fantasy.
He will not believe that we saw it twice!
By standing watch with us tonight, he can
See it for himself.

HORATIO: It will not appear.

BERNARDO: Sit down awhile,
And let us once again tell you about
What we have seen two nights in a row.
Last night, about this same time,
The clock was striking one—

MARCELLUS: Quiet! It's coming again!

(The **Ghost** enters, dressed in armor.)

BERNARDO: It looks just like the dead King!

MARCELLUS: Speak to it, Horatio!

HORATIO *(to the Ghost)*: Who are you?
Why do you wear the armor in which
Our buried King did sometimes march?
By heaven, I order you to speak!

MARCELLUS: It seems to be offended.

BERNARDO: See, it stalks away!

HORATIO: Stay! Speak! I order you, speak!

(The **Ghost** exits.)

MARCELLUS: It will not answer. It is gone.

BERNARDO: What do you think now, Horatio?
You tremble and look pale.

Isn't this something more than fantasy?

HORATIO: Before my God,

I would never have believed it

Unless I saw it with my own eyes.

MARCELLUS: Isn't it like the King?

HORATIO: As like as you are to yourself!

That was the very armor he had on when

He fought the ambitious King of Norway.

And he frowned just like that once,

When angry. It is strange.

I have no idea what to think.

But it seems like a bad sign.

MARCELLUS: Tell me, if you know,

Why this quiet and watchful ghost

Has come here these past nights.

And why does our country seem

To be preparing for war?

HORATIO: I'll tell what I've heard.

Our last King, whose image just appeared,

Killed King Fortinbras of Norway.

Along with his life,

Fortinbras lost all the lands

He had risked in the battle.
If Fortinbras had won, our good King
Would have had to give up his lands.
That was their agreement, so it was only fair.
Now, sir, young Fortinbras, his son,
Rash, hot, and foolish,
Has raised an army of lawless men
To recover the land lost by his father.
This must be why we are preparing for war,
And the reason we must keep watch at night.

BERNARDO: I think you must be right.

HORATIO: Quiet! Look! Here it comes again!

(The **Ghost** enters again.)

Stay, illusion! If you have any use of voice,
Speak to me. If I may help you in any way,
Speak to me. If you know anything about
Your country's fate, which,
By knowing in advance, we may avoid,
Oh, speak!

(A rooster crows. The **Ghost** exits.)

BERNARDO: It was about to speak,
When the rooster crowed.

HORATIO: I have heard that spirits

    Must leave the earth during the day,

    And what we just saw proves that story!

    The sun is rising. Our watch is over.

    Let us report what we have seen tonight

    To young Hamlet. I think that

    This spirit, silent to us, will speak to him.

MARCELLUS: Let's do it. I know where he is.

(**All** exit.)

Scene ❷ ⌢₄

(**King Claudius**, **Queen Gertrude**, **Prince Hamlet**, **Polonius**, **Laertes**, **Voltimand**, **Cornelius**, **Lords**, and **Attendants** enter a room of state in the castle at Elsinore.)

KING: The memory of our dear brother's death
Is still fresh. Our hearts are full of grief.
Yet, we must think of our kingdom,
Which needs a leader in this warlike time.
Therefore we have taken as wife
Our former sister-in-law.
Now, as you know, young Fortinbras
Thinks that we are weak. He thinks that
Our late dear brother's death
Has left our state in confusion and chaos.
Thinking he has an advantage, he has been
Pestering us to surrender those lands
Lost by his father to our brother.
That is the reason for this meeting.
We have written to the King of Norway,
The uncle of young Fortinbras.
He is sick and bedridden. He knows little
Of his nephew's actions. We asked him

To order his nephew to leave us alone.
We want you, Cornelius and Voltimand,
To take this letter to the King of Norway.
Now farewell—and do your duty quickly!

(King Claudius hands them a letter.)

CORNELIUS AND VOLTIMAND: Yes, my lord.

(**They** bow and exit.)

KING: Now, Laertes, what's the news with you?
You mentioned a request. What is it?

LAERTES: My good lord, I ask your permission
To return to France. I came here willingly
To show my support for your coronation.
Now, I must confess, that duty done,
My wishes bend again toward France.

KING: Do you have your father's permission?
What does Polonius say?

POLONIUS: My lord, he has my permission.

KING: Enjoy your youth, Laertes. Time is yours,
And you may spend it as you like!
But now, my nephew Hamlet, and my son—

HAMLET *(aside):* I may be your nephew,
But I will never be your son!

KING: Why are you still so gloomy?

QUEEN: Good Hamlet, cast off your dark mood.
You know that all living things must die,
Passing through nature to eternity.

HAMLET: Yes, madam, I know.

KING: It is sweet of you, Hamlet,
To mourn this way for your father.
But, your father lost a father.
And that lost father also lost his.
You must mourn for a time. But to keep on
Mourning so long is stubborn and unmanly.
It shows a weak heart, an impatient mind.
It is a fault against heaven, against the dead,
And against nature. Please stop grieving.
Think of us as a father. Let all see that
You are heir to the throne, and I love you
No less than the dearest father loves his son!
Your wish to return to school in Wittenberg
Goes against our wishes. We ask you to stay
Here in the cheer and comfort of our eye,
Our chief courtier, nephew, and our son.

QUEEN: Please, Hamlet, stay here with us.

HAMLET: I shall obey you, Mother.

KING: Why, it is a loving and fair reply.

(to the Queen): Madam, come.

(**All** exit but Hamlet.)

HAMLET: Oh, that this too, too solid flesh
Would melt, thaw, and turn into a dew!
Or if only suicide were not a sin!
Oh, God! Oh, God!
How weary, stale, flat, and useless
The world seems! It is an unweeded garden,
Gone to seed. That it should come to this!
Not even two months dead, so fine a king!
He loved my mother so much that
He wouldn't allow the wind to blow too hard
On her face. She would hang on him
As if her appetite grew by what it fed on.
Yet, within a month—let me not think of it!
Frailty, your name is woman!
Oh, God! A beast with no power to reason
Would have mourned longer! Now,
Married to my uncle—my father's brother—
But no more like my father

Than I am like Hercules. Within a month,
Before the salt of her tears had left her eyes,
She married. Oh, most wicked speed!
This marriage can come to no good.
But break, my heart—I must hold my tongue!

(**Horatio**, **Marcellus**, and **Bernardo** enter.)

HORATIO: Hail to your lordship!

HAMLET: Hello, Horatio! What brought you
Here from Wittenberg?

HORATIO: I came to see your father's funeral.

HAMLET: Do not mock me, fellow student.
I think it was to see my mother's wedding.

HORATIO: Indeed, it followed soon after.

HAMLET: Thrift, Horatio! The funeral meats
Were served cold at the marriage tables.
I wish I had never seen that day, Horatio!
My father!—I think I see my father.

HORATIO *(surprised)*: Where, my lord?

HAMLET: In my mind's eye, Horatio.

HORATIO: I saw him once. He was a good king.

HAMLET: He was a man, all in all.
I shall not look upon his like again.

HORATIO: My lord, I think I saw him last night.

HAMLET: Saw who?

HORATIO: My lord . . . the king, your father.

HAMLET: My father? Let me hear!

HORATIO: Yes. Listen, I will tell you about it.
　　For two nights, Marcellus and Bernardo
　　Saw a figure like your father,
　　Dressed from head to toe in armor.
　　They told me about it in secret.
　　I kept watch with them the third night.
　　The ghostly figure came.
　　I knew your father. It looked just like him.

HAMLET: Did you speak to it?

HORATIO: I did, but it did not answer.

HAMLET: It is very strange.

HORATIO: As I live, my honored lord, it is true.
　　We thought it our duty to let you know of it.

HAMLET: Indeed, sirs—but it troubles me.
　　Are you on watch tonight?

MARCELLUS AND BERNARDO: We are, my lord.

HAMLET: He was dressed in armor, you say?

BOTH: Yes, my lord.

HAMLET: Then you did not see his face?

HORATIO: We did. He wore the visor up.

HAMLET: Was he frowning?

HORATIO: His face was more sad than angry.

HAMLET: I wish I had been there!

> I will watch with you tonight.
>
> Perhaps it will walk again. If it looks like
>
> My noble father, I'll speak to it.
>
> Do not tell anyone else about this.
>
> I'll see you tonight, between 11 and 12.

ALL: Until then, farewell.

(**Horatio**, **Marcellus**, and **Bernardo** exit.)

HAMLET: My father's spirit—in arms! All is not well.

> I wish night had already come! Until then,
>
> Be still, my soul. Foul deeds will rise,
>
> Though the earth hides them from our eyes.

(**Hamlet** exits.)

Scene ❸ 🎧

(**Laertes** and **Ophelia** enter a room in Polonius's house.)

LAERTES: My bags are on board. Farewell.

And, sister, please write to me.

OPHELIA: Do you doubt that I would?

LAERTES: As for Hamlet, and his affections,

Do not expect too much.

They are like violets in the spring,

Fast-growing and sweet, but not lasting,

The perfume of a minute. No more.

OPHELIA: No more than that?

LAERTES: No. Perhaps he loves you now.

But be careful. Remember his position.

His will is not his own.

Unlike other people, he may not do as he wishes.

The safety and well-being

Of this whole state depend on his choices.

Therefore, he must first consider Denmark

Before he can choose a wife.

If he says he loves you, keep all this in mind.

If you lose your heart or your honor,

You might also lose your good reputation.

Fear it, Ophelia. Fear it, my dear sister.

Be careful of the danger of desire.

OPHELIA: I shall take your words to heart.

But, my good brother, do not show me

The steep and thorny way to heaven

If you don't take your own advice.

(**Polonius** enters.)

POLONIUS: Still here, Laertes? Aboard! Aboard!

The wind sits in the shoulder of your sail,

And you are keeping everyone waiting.

(laying his hand on Laertes's head): There!

My blessing on you! Here is some advice.

Be friendly, but by no means vulgar.

Keep those friends you have, and

Tie them to your soul with hoops of steel.

But do not give the hand of friendship

Too easily to every new person you meet.

Give every man your ear, but few your voice.

Listen to criticism, but do not judge others.

Buy clothes as costly as you can afford—

Good quality, but not gaudy—

For a man's clothing tells a lot about him.

Neither a borrower nor a lender be,

For a loan can lose both itself and the friend,

And borrowing dulls the edge of thrift.

This above all: To your own self be true,

And it must follow, as the night the day,

You cannot then be false to any man.

Farewell. My blessings go with you!

LAERTES: I humbly take my leave, my lord.

(to Ophelia): Farewell, Ophelia. Remember

What I have said to you.

OPHELIA: It is locked in my memory,

And you yourself shall keep the key to it.

(**Laertes** exits.)

POLONIUS: What did he say to you, Ophelia?

OPHELIA: Something about the Lord Hamlet.

POLONIUS: I thought so.

I'm told that you and Hamlet

Have been spending much time alone lately.

If this is so, I must tell you that you do not

Understand what people might be saying.

What is between you? Tell me the truth.

OPHELIA: My lord, he has let me know

That he feels affection toward me.

POLONIUS: Affection? Ha! Are you fool enough
To believe him?

OPHELIA: He has courted me honorably
And has supported his words
With almost all the holy vows of heaven.

POLONIUS: Such vows are like traps for birds.
Do not take him seriously. From now on,
You must not be so available. In fact,
Do not spend any time alone with him.
I don't want you to even talk to him.
That's an order. Change your ways.

OPHELIA: I shall obey, my lord.

(**Polonius** and **Ophelia** exit.)

Scene 4

(**Hamlet**, **Horatio**, and **Marcellus** enter an area before the castle.)

HAMLET: The air seems to bite. It is very cold.
What is the hour?

HORATIO: I think it is almost 12.

MARCELLUS: No, it is past midnight.

HORATIO: Indeed? Then it is almost the time
That the spirit has been coming to walk.

(The **Ghost** enters.)

HORATIO: Look, my lord, it comes!

HAMLET: May the angels defend us!
Whether you mean us evil or good,
I will speak to you. I'll call you Hamlet, King,
Father, Royal Dane.
Oh, answer me! Tell why your holy bones
Have burst their burial clothes.
Why has your tomb opened its marble jaws
To cast you up again? What does this mean,
That you rise up to visit in full armor?
Say, why is this? What should we do?

(The **Ghost** motions to **Hamlet**.)

HORATIO: It beckons you to draw nearer.

MARCELLUS: Do not go after it!

HORATIO: No, by no means.

HAMLET: It will not speak unless I follow it.

HORATIO: Do not, my lord.

HAMLET: Why, what should I fear?
My life is not worth the price of a pin.
And for my soul, what can it do to that?
It waves me forth again. I'll follow it.

HORATIO: What if it leads you toward danger
Or into madness? Beware!

HAMLET: It waves to me still.
(to the Ghost): Go on. I'll follow you.

MARCELLUS *(holding him back)*: You shall not go,
my lord.

HAMLET: Hold off your hands.

HORATIO: Listen to us. You shall not go.

HAMLET: My fate cries out,
And makes each vein in this body
As brave as a lion.

(The **Ghost** beckons.)

Let go, gentlemen.

(breaking free): I'll make a ghost of anyone
Who tries to stop me! I say, away!

(to the Ghost): Go on. I'll follow you.

(The **Ghost** and **Hamlet** exit.)

MARCELLUS: Let us go after him.

HORATIO: What good will that do?

MARCELLUS: Something is rotten in the state of
Denmark.

HORATIO: Heaven will take care of it!

MARCELLUS: No, let's follow him.

(**Horatio** and **Marcellus** exit.)

Scene 5 🎧

(The **Ghost** and **Hamlet** enter a more remote part of the castle.)

HAMLET: Where will you lead me?
    Speak! I'll go no further.

GHOST: Listen to me.

HAMLET: I will.

GHOST: The hour is almost come, when I must
    Give myself up to the tormenting flames.

HAMLET: Alas, poor ghost!

GHOST: Do not pity me, but listen
    To what I shall tell you.

HAMLET: Speak! I am bound to hear.

GHOST: And when you hear, you will be
    Bound to revenge.

HAMLET: What?

GHOST: I am your father's spirit—
    Doomed for a certain term to walk the night,
    And for the day confined to wasting fires
    Till the foul crimes done in my life
    Are burned away. If I were not forbidden

To tell the secrets of my prison-house,
I could tell a tale whose lightest word
Would freeze your young blood. It would
Make your eyes pop from their sockets, and
Your hair stand up like a porcupine's quills.
But this eternal tale must not be heard
By ears of flesh and blood. Oh, listen!
If you did ever love your dear father—

HAMLET: Oh, God!

GHOST: Avenge his foul and most unnatural murder.

HAMLET: Murder!

GHOST: Murder most foul, as murder always is.
But this was most foul, strange, and unnatural.

HAMLET: Tell me what happened, so that I,
With wings as swift as thoughts of love,
May sweep to my revenge.

GHOST: Hamlet, hear what I say.
The story is being told that a serpent
Stung me as I was sleeping in my orchard.
All Denmark has been told this lie.
But know, noble youth,
The serpent that did sting your father's life
Now wears his crown.

HAMLET: Oh, it's just as I thought! My uncle!

GHOST: Yes, that beast.
First he won to his shameful lust
The will of my queen. Oh, Hamlet,
What a fall that was for her!
From me, whose love was sacred and true,
To that wretch who is so far below me!
But quickly: I think I smell the morning air.
I will be brief. I was sleeping in my orchard,

As was my custom in the afternoon,

When your uncle stole in upon me

And poured poison in my ear.

The poison he used was swift as quicksilver.

It coursed through my whole body

And killed me almost in an instant.

Thus, as I was sleeping, I was killed

By my own brother's hand. In one moment,

I was deprived of life, of crown, of queen.

Cut off even before I could confess my sins.

I was sent to my maker

With all my imperfections on my head.

Oh, horrible! Oh, horrible! Most horrible!

If you have any feelings in you, bear it not.

Do not let the royal bed of Denmark be

A couch for luxury and evil incest. But

Whatever you do, do not harm your mother.

Leave her to heaven and to those thorns

That lie in her heart to prick and sting her.

Farewell at once! It is almost morning.

Goodbye, goodbye! Hamlet, remember me!

(The **Ghost** exits.)

HAMLET: Remember you!

Yes, you poor ghost! From my memory,
I'll wipe away all foolish records,
All advice from books, all past pressures
That youth and observation put there.
Your commandment alone shall live
Within my brain, unmixed with lesser
Matter. Oh, most evil woman!
Oh, villain, villain, smiling, evil villain!
One may smile, and smile, and be a villain.
At least, I am sure, it may be so in Denmark.
So, Uncle, there you are. Now to my promise:
"Remember me." I have sworn it.

HORATIO *(from offstage)*: My lord, my lord!

MARCELLUS *(from offstage)*: Lord Hamlet!

HORATIO *(from offstage)*: Heaven help him!

(**Horatio** and **Marcellus** enter.)

MARCELLUS: What happened, my noble lord?

HORATIO: What news, my lord?

HAMLET: Oh, wonderful!

 HORATIO: My good lord, tell us.

HAMLET: No, you will reveal it.

HORATIO: Not I, my lord, by heaven!

MARCELLUS: Nor I, my lord.

HAMLET: Then you'll keep a secret?

HORATIO AND MARCELLUS: Yes, my lord.

HAMLET: There's a villain living in Denmark.

HORATIO: We don't need a ghost, my lord,
 Come from the grave to tell us this.

HAMLET: Why, you are right.
 And so, let us shake hands and part.
 You go about your business,
 And I'll go about mine. Now, good friends,
 As you are friends, scholars, and soldiers,
 Grant me one poor request.

HORATIO: What is it, my lord? We will.

HAMLET: Never make known what you have
 Seen tonight.

HORATIO AND MARCELLUS: We will not.

HAMLET: Swear it, upon my sword.

MARCELLUS: We have sworn, my lord, already.

HAMLET: Indeed, upon my sword, indeed.

ACT 1
SCENE 5

GHOST *(from beneath the stage)*: Swear.

HAMLET: Come on!

You hear this fellow in the cellar? Swear.

HORATIO: State the oath, my lord.

HAMLET: Never to speak of what you have seen,

Swear by my sword.

GHOST *(from beneath)*: Swear.

HAMLET: Come here, gentlemen,

And lay your hands again upon my sword.

Never to speak of what you have heard,

Swear by my sword.

GHOST *(from beneath)*: Swear.

HAMLET: Well said, old mole!

Once more, good friends.

HORATIO: Oh, this is very strange!

HAMLET: And therefore, as a stranger, welcome it.

There are more things in heaven and earth,

Horatio, than are dreamt of in your philosophy.

But come here, as before. Swear.

GHOST *(from beneath)*: Swear.

HAMLET: Rest, rest, troubled spirit!

(**Horatio** and **Marcellus** swear.)

So, gentlemen,

With all my love I do thank you.

Let us go in together.

And, remember, not a word.

The time is out of joint. Oh, cursed spite! That

ever I was born to set it right!

Now, come, let's go together.

(**All** exit.)

ACT 2

Summary

歐菲莉亞告訴波隆尼爾有關哈姆雷特近日的怪異舉動,波隆尼爾認為哈姆雷特是因為對歐菲莉亞求愛不成而得了心病,決定將此事稟告國王與皇后。國王與皇后派羅生克蘭和蓋登思鄧監視哈姆雷特,並查出其行事怪異之因。

康尼留斯和傅特曼從挪威回來,並報告小福丁布拉已答應不再攻打挪威,轉攻波蘭。當波隆尼爾報告哈姆雷特對歐菲莉亞的迷戀後,克勞地和葛簇特同意這也許是哈姆雷特舉止特異的誘因。克勞地和波隆尼爾決定偷聽哈姆雷特與歐菲莉亞的會面情況。羅生克蘭和蓋登思鄧接著再次出場,而哈姆雷特已發現這兩人是被派到城堡監視他的。他們提到有組巡演演員將在城堡進行戲劇表演,哈姆雷特要求演員在戲中加入幾句他寫的新台詞,認為國王將對這些台詞有所反應,並證明他有罪。

Scene 1

(**Polonius** and **Reynaldo** enter a room in Polonius's house.)

POLONIUS: Before you visit Laertes, find out
What other people are saying about him.
You might start by saying something
Like this: "I know Laertes a little,
But not well. He seems to be very wild,
Addicted to such and such." And then you
Could name whatever vices you please, but
None so bad as to dishonor him.

REYNALDO: Such as gambling, my lord?

POLONIUS: Yes, or drinking and fighting,
The common wildness of young men.
Speak of his faults in such a way that
They may seem very minor,
The flash and outbreak of a fiery mind.
As you speak of my son's slight faults,
The person you're speaking to might say,
"I know the gentleman. I saw him yesterday,
Or the other day, or then, or then,
With such, or such. And, as you say,

There he was gambling." Listen, now,
Your bait of falsehood takes this fish of truth.
I just want to know what he's been doing.
Do you understand me?

REYNALDO: I do, my lord.

POLONIUS: Farewell now. Keep an eye on him.

(**Reynaldo** exits. **Ophelia** enters.)

POLONIUS: Ophelia! What's the matter?

OPHELIA: Oh, Father, I am so frightened!

POLONIUS: With what, in the name of God?

OPHELIA: As I was sewing in my room,
Lord Hamlet came in, his shirt unbuttoned.
He wore no hat, and his socks were dirty
And falling down to his ankles.
He had a horrible look on his face.
He seemed out of his mind.

POLONIUS: Mad for your love?

OPHELIA: My lord, I do not know.
But it seemed that way.

POLONIUS: What did he say?

OPHELIA: He held me hard by the wrist.
Then he stared directly into my face,

As if he wanted to draw it. For a long time,
He stayed like this. At last, he shook my arm,
Raised a pitiful sigh, and let me go.
Then, with his head turned over his shoulder,
He found his way out without using his eyes,
For he left my room without their help,
And, to the last, kept his eyes on me.

POLONIUS: Come with me to tell the king.
This kind of love is dangerous.
It can lead one to desperate deeds.
Have you given him any hard words lately?

OPHELIA: No, my good lord.
But, as you ordered, I've refused his letters
And have spent no time with him.

POLONIUS: That has driven him mad.
I am sorry that I misjudged him.
I thought he was toying with you and
Meant to ruin you. Maybe I am too jealous!

Let us see the king. We must tell him.
If this is kept secret, it could lead
To more grief than any of us need.

(**Ophelia** and **Polonius** exit.)

Scene 2

(The **King**, the **Queen**, **Rosencrantz**, **Guildenstern**, and **attendants** enter a room in the castle.)

KING: Welcome, dear Rosencrantz and
Guildenstern! We have missed you!
We asked you to come so quickly because
We need a favor from you. You have heard
Something about the changes in Hamlet.
He is different both inside and out.
The reason—other than his father's death—
I cannot imagine.
You two are close to his age and have been
Brought up with him since childhood.
I ask you both to stay here in our court
For a short time. Spend time with him.
Maybe you can find out what is wrong.
If we knew, perhaps we could help him.

QUEEN: Gentlemen, he has talked about you.
I am sure there are no two men living
That he likes any better than you.
If it will please you to spend some time here,
Your visit will be royally rewarded.

ROSENCRANTZ: No reward is necessary.

GUILDENSTERN: We are happy to help.

KING: Thank you, Rosencrantz and
Gentle Guildenstern.

QUEEN: Thank you, Guildenstern and
Gentle Rosencrantz. I beg you to visit
My too-much-changed son at once.

(**Rosencrantz** and **Guildenstern** exit. **Polonius**
enters.)

POLONIUS: My good lord, the ambassadors
From Norway have joyfully returned .

KING: You have always brought good news!

POLONIUS: Have I, my lord? I assure you,
Majesty, that my duty is as sacred to me
As my soul. And I think I have found
The very cause of Hamlet's madness.

KING: Oh, speak of that. I long to hear it!

POLONIUS: First, talk to the ambassadors.
My news shall be dessert to that great feast.

KING: Very well. Bring them in.

(**Polonius** exits.)

(to the Queen): He tells me that he knows
Why Hamlet has been behaving so strangely.

QUEEN: I thought the reasons were clear—
His father's death and our quick marriage.

KING: Well, let us hear what Polonius says.

(**Polonius** enters, with **Voltimand** and **Cornelius**.)

Welcome, my good friends! Say, Voltimand,
What news do you have from Norway?

VOLTIMAND: The King of Norway thought
That his nephew was preparing for war
With Poland. But as he looked into it,
He found it was truly against your highness.
Then he ordered young Fortinbras to stop.
In brief, Fortinbras obeys and vows
Never to take arms against your majesty.
At this, the overjoyed King of Norway
Gave him enough money to take his soldiers
Against Poland.

(Voltimand gives the king a paper.)

The King of Norway asks your permission
For his nephew to march through your lands
On his way to Poland.

KING: When we have more time,

We'll read, answer, and think about this.

Meantime, we thank you for your efforts.

Rest now. Tonight, we'll feast together.

(**Voltimand** and **Cornelius** exit.)

POLONIUS: That was good news!

And now, since brevity is the soul of wit,

I will be brief: Your noble son is mad.

It is true that it is a pity,

And a pity it is that it is true.

But, to get to the point—

Let us agree that he is mad.

Now we must find out the cause of this effect,

Or, rather, the cause of this defect.

My daughter has given me this.

(Polonius holds up a letter.)

Now, listen and think about it. (reading)

"To the heavenly, and my soul's idol,

The most beautified Ophelia"—

(He comments on the letter.)

That's a stupid word, a vile word.

"Beautified" is a vile word. But listen.

41

(reading again): "Doubt that the stars are fire.
Doubt that the sun does move.
Doubt truth to be a liar.
But never doubt that I love.
Oh, Ophelia, I am not very good at this.
But please believe that I love you best.
Oh, most best, believe it. Farewell.
I am yours forever, dear lady. Hamlet."
(He folds up the letter.)

In obedience, my daughter showed me this .

KING: But how has she received his love?

POLONIUS: Well, when I first found out about it,
I went right away and told my daughter,
"Lord Hamlet is a prince, out of your reach.
This must not be." And then I told her
That she should lock herself away from him,
Admit no messengers, receive no gifts.
She took my advice. He fell into a sadness,
Then into a fast, then into a weakness,
Then into a lightness. In this way, he fell into
The madness that all of us now mourn.

KING: Do you think this is the reason?

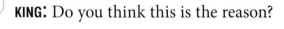

QUEEN: It may be. It's very likely.

POLONIUS: Have I ever been wrong before?

KING: Not that I know.

How may we test your idea?

POLONIUS: You know sometimes he walks

For hours at a time here in the lobby.

QUEEN: So he does, indeed.

POLONIUS: At such a time, I'll make sure that

My daughter is nearby.

You and I will hide behind the drapes and

Watch their meeting . If he does not love her,

And has not gone mad because of it, then

I'll quit my job and be a farmer!

KING: We will try it.

(**Hamlet** enters, reading a book.)

QUEEN: See how sadly he comes, reading.

POLONIUS: Go away, I beg you, both of you.

I'll speak to him presently. Please leave.

(The **King**, the **Queen**, and **attendants** exit.)

How are you, my good Lord Hamlet?

HAMLET: I am well, thanks to God.

POLONIUS: Do you know me, my lord?

HAMLET: Yes. You are a sly fishmonger.

POLONIUS: Not I, my lord.

HAMLET: Then I wish you were that honest.

POLONIUS: Honest, my lord?

HAMLET: Yes, sir. In this world, an honest man Is one in ten thousand.

POLONIUS: That's very true, my lord.

HAMLET: Do you have a daughter?

POLONIUS: I have, my lord.

HAMLET: Do not let her walk in the sun. She could get hurt if she goes outside.

POLONIUS: What do you mean by that?

(aside): Still talking about my daughter. Yet he did not know me at first. He thought I sold fish. He is far gone. Truly, in my youth, I suffered for love in much the same way. I'll speak to him again .

(to Hamlet): What do you read, my lord?

HAMLET: Words, words, words .

POLONIUS: What is the matter, my lord?

HAMLET: Between who?

POLONIUS: I mean, the matter that you read.

HAMLET: Lies, sir! The writer says here that old men have gray beards, that their faces are wrinkled, and that their eyes are runny. He also says they lack brains and have weak legs. All of this, sir, I most strongly believe, yet I don't think it should be written down.

POLONIUS *(aside)*: Though this be madness, yet there is a method in it . *(to Hamlet)*: My lord, I must most humbly take leave of you.

HAMLET: Sir, you cannot take from me anything that I will more willingly give—except my life, except my life, except my life . . .

POLONIUS: Farewell, my lord.

(**Polonius** exits.)

HAMLET: These tiresome old fools!

(**Rosencrantz** and **Guildenstern** enter.)

HAMLET: Good lads, what's the news?

ROSENCRANTZ: None, my lord, but that the world's grown honest .

HAMLET: Then the end of time must be near! But your news is not true. Let me ask you a question. What have you ever done to Fortune that she sends you to prison here?

GUILDENSTERN: Prison, my lord?

HAMLET: Denmark is a prison.

ROSENCRANTZ: Then the world is one.

HAMLET: A big one, with many rooms and dungeons, Denmark being the worst.

ROSENCRANTZ: We do not think so, my lord.

HAMLET: Why, then, it is not a prison to you! For there is nothing either good or bad unless you think it so. To me, it is a prison.

ROSENCRANTZ: Then your ambition makes it one. Denmark is too narrow for your mind.

HAMLET: Oh, God, I could live in a nutshell, and count myself a king of infinite space —except that I have bad dreams.

GUILDENSTERN: Those dreams, indeed, are ambition, for ambition is merely the shadow of a dream.

HAMLET: A dream itself is but a shadow.

ROSENCRANTZ: Truly. And I believe that ambition is so light and airy that it is but a shadow's shadow.

HAMLET: Shall we go to the court? For, truly, I cannot think about this anymore.

ROSENCRANTZ AND GUILDENSTERN: We'll wait upon you.

HAMLET: No, you won't. I will not group you with the rest of my servants. To tell the truth, I am most dreadfully waited upon. But, in the familiar way of friendship, what brings you here to Elsinore?

ROSENCRANTZ: To visit you. No other reason.

HAMLET: Thank you. But, really, dear friends, were you not sent for? Come, tell me the truth. Come, come. Speak to me!

GUILDENSTERN: What should we say, my lord?

HAMLET: Why, anything—but answer the question. You were sent for, weren't you? I know the king and queen sent for you.

ROSENCRANTZ: For what reason, my lord?

HAMLET: You tell me. In the name of our

friendship, be truthful with me.
Were you sent for or not?

GUILDENSTERN: My lord, we were sent for.

HAMLET: I will tell you why, so you won't have to break your secrecy with the king and queen. I have lately—but I don't know why—lost all joy and stopped exercising. Indeed, I feel so bad that the earth seems to me a sterile place. This most excellent air—why, it seems no more to me than a foul collection of vapors. What a piece of work is man! How noble in reason! How infinite in mind! In shape and motion, how admirable! In action, how like an angel! In understanding, how like a god! The beauty of the world! The highest of animals! And yet to me, what is this piece of dust? Man does not delight me, no. Nor does woman, though by your smiling you seem to say so.

ROSENCRANTZ: I had no such thoughts.

HAMLET: Why did you laugh, then, when I said "Man does not delight me"?

ROSENCRANTZ: I was thinking, my lord, if man
does not delight you, the actors who are
coming will get a weak welcome.

HAMLET: Which actors are they?

ROSENCRANTZ: The ones you like so much—the
tragedy-actors from the city.

HAMLET: Why are they traveling? In the city,
they seemed to be doing well, in reputation
and profit. Are they still as well-liked as
they were when I was there?

ROSENCRANTZ: No, indeed, they are not.

HAMLET: Why? Have they grown rusty?

ROSENCRANTZ: No, they are still good. But there is
a new group of child actors. They are very
popular now. They are quite in fashion.

HAMLET: You say they are children? Who takes
care of them? How are they fed? Will they
quit acting when their voices change? Will
they say later, when they grow into common
actors, that their writers do them wrong?

ROSENCRANTZ: There has been much talk about
it. No one knows how the argument will be

resolved. Still, that is why the tragedy-actors
are on the road now.

(Trumpets from offstage announce the actors.)

GUILDENSTERN: Here come the players.

HAMLET: Gentlemen, you are welcome to Elsinore.
But my uncle-father and aunt-mother are
deceived about me.

GUILDENSTERN: In what way, my dear lord?

HAMLET: I am but mad north-northwest. When the
wind is from the south, I know a hawk from a
handsaw!

(**Polonius** enters.)

POLONIUS: Greetings, gentlemen!

HAMLET *(aside to Rosencrantz and Guildenstern):*
That great baby you see there is not yet out of
his baby clothes.

ROSENCRANTZ *(aside to Hamlet):* Perhaps the old
man is in his second childhood.

HAMLET *(aside):* I predict that he comes to tell me of
the actors. Listen.

(to Polonius): Greetings, sir.

POLONIUS: My lord, the actors are here.

HAMLET: Is that so?

POLONIUS: Upon my honor.

(**Four or five actors** enter.)

HAMLET: Welcome, gentlemen! Welcome, all!
(to Polonius): My good lord, will you see that
the players have good rooms? Let them
make themselves comfortable.

POLONIUS: My lord, I will. Come, sirs.

HAMLET: Follow him, friends. We'll hear a play
tomorrow.

(**Polonius** exits, with all the **actors** but the first.
Hamlet speaks to the remaining actor.)

HAMLET: Can you play "The Murder of Gonzago"?

FIRST ACTOR: Yes, my lord.

HAMLET: We'll have it tomorrow night. You
could, if I needed it, study a speech of some
12 or 16 lines, which I'll write and add to
the play, couldn't you?

FIRST ACTOR: Yes, my lord.

HAMLET: Very well. *(pointing where Polonius has
exited)*: Follow that lord, and see that you do
not mock him.

(**First actor** exits. Hamlet speaks to Rosencrantz and Guildenstern.)

I'll see you tonight. Welcome to Elsinore.

ROSENCRANTZ: Thank you, my good lord.

(**Rosencrantz** and **Guildenstern** exit.)

HAMLET: Now I am alone.

Oh, what a rogue I am! Am I a coward?
I must be, or I would have fed all the birds
With the king's body—that bloody villain!
Oh, revenge!
I, the son of a dear father murdered,
Prompted to my revenge by heaven and hell,
Must unpack my heart with words.
Well, I have heard that guilty creatures,
Sitting at a play, have been struck to the soul
By a scene reminding them of their own acts.
Sometimes they are prompted to admit
Their evil actions. I'll have these actors
Play something like my father's murder
Before my uncle. I'll observe his looks.
If he reacts, I'll know what to do.
The ghost I have seen may be the devil.
I know the devil can take a pleasing shape.

Perhaps, due to my weakness and sadness,
He is leading me down an evil path.
I want to trust the ghost—but I can't be sure
That it was my father's spirit.
I need more proof. The play's the thing
In which I'll catch the conscience of the king.

(**Hamlet** exits.)

ACT 3

Summary

羅生克蘭和蓋登思鄧向國王和皇后稟報，哈姆雷特希望國王和皇后柳人當晚前往觀賞戲劇演出。國王和波隆尼爾偷聽到哈姆雷特對歐菲莉亞表示，他從未愛過她。當晚，當演員演出哈姆雷特寫的新橋段，哈姆雷特發現國王對此感到十分憤怒。該場戲與其父王被謀殺一事十分相像，當國王突然憤而離席，哈姆雷特與赫瑞修確信國王曾犯下罪行。

羅生克蘭和蓋登思鄧上場，告訴哈姆雷特，皇后想見他。當哈姆雷特來找皇后時，波隆尼爾正躲在皇后的寢室，哈姆雷特聽見聲音以為那是國王隔著簾幕一劍刺死波隆尼爾。先王的鬼魂再度出現，請哈姆雷特對母后在言行上更加溫和，接著哈姆雷特下場，並拖走波隆尼爾的屍體。

Scene ❶ 🎧

(The **King**, the **Queen**, **Polonius**, **Ophelia**, **Rosencrantz**, and **Guildenstern** enter a room in the castle.)

KING: Didn't Hamlet tell you why he has been
　　Acting so strange?

ROSENCRANTZ: He says that he feels distracted,
　　But he will not speak of the cause.

QUEEN: Was he interested in any pastime?

ROSENCRANTZ: Madam, it so happened that
　　We passed some actors on our way here.
　　We told him about this,
　　And there did seem in him a kind of joy
　　To hear of it. They are at the castle now,
　　And I think they have already been ordered
　　To play before him tonight.

POLONIUS: It is true. He asked me to invite
　　Your Majesties to attend the play tonight.

KING: With all my heart, I am very happy
　　To hear that he is interested in something.
　　Gentlemen, tell him that we will be there.

ROSENCRANTZ: We shall, my lord.

(**Rosencrantz** and **Guildenstern** exit.)

KING: Sweet Gertrude, leave us, too.

We have sent for Hamlet so that he,

As if by accident, may meet Ophelia here.

Her father and I—lawful spies—

Will watch them

Without being seen. We wish to judge,

By the way he acts, if he is in love or not.

QUEEN: I shall obey you.

(to Ophelia): As for you, Ophelia, I do wish

That your beauty is the happy cause of

Hamlet's wildness. I also hope your virtues

Will bring him back to himself again—

For the honor of you both.

OPHELIA: Madam, I wish the same.

(The **Queen** exits.)

POLONIUS: Ophelia, walk over here.

Read from this book of prayers

So it won't seem strange that you are alone.

(to the King): I hear him coming!

(The **King** and **Polonius** exit. **Hamlet** enters.)

HAMLET: To be, or not to be—

That is the question. Is it nobler in the mind

To suffer the slings and arrows

Of outrageous fortune? Or is it better

To take arms against a sea of troubles,

And by fighting, end them?

To die is to sleep—no more than that.

By this sleep we say we end the heartaches

And the thousand natural shocks

That flesh must suffer. It is an end

Warmly to be wished. To die is to sleep.

To sleep . . . perhaps to dream.

Ay, there's the rub. For in the sleep of death,

What dreams may come?

These thoughts must make us pause.

Why bear the whips and scorns of time?

Why suffer the pangs of unhappy love and

The proud man's insults,

When we might end them with a dagger?

It is because we dread what might happen

After death, that undiscovered country

From which no traveler returns.

This dread puzzles the will.

It makes us prefer to bear those ills we have

Rather than fly to others we do not know.
Thus conscience makes cowards of us all.
(He sees Ophelia.) The fair Ophelia!
In your prayers, remember my sins.

OPHELIA: My lord, I have gifts of yours that
I would like to return. Please take them.

HAMLET: No, not I. I never gave you anything.

OPHELIA: You know right well you did.
And with them such sweet words that made
The things richer. Their perfume now lost,
Take them back. For, to the noble mind,
Rich gifts turn poor when givers are unkind.

HAMLET: I did love you once.

OPHELIA: You made me believe so.

HAMLET: You should not have believed me. I
loved you not!

OPHELIA: Then I was truly deceived.

HAMLET: Go to a nunnery! Why should you
become a mother of sinners? Why should
such fellows as I be crawling between
earth and heaven? We are all scoundrels,
all of us. Believe none of us. Go to a

nunnery! But if you do marry, I'll give you this advice: If you are as chaste as ice, as pure as snow, you will not escape slander. Be off to a nunnery!

OPHELIA: Heavenly powers, restore him!

HAMLET: Or, if you must marry, marry a fool. Wise men know well enough how wicked you might be. I say, we will have no more marriages. Those who are married already, all but one, shall live. The rest shall keep as they are. To a nunnery—go!

(**Hamlet** exits.)

OPHELIA: What a noble mind has lost its reason!
And I, the most wretched of ladies.
I heard the sweet music of his loving words.
Now that music is out of tune and harsh.
Oh, woe is me, to have seen
What I have seen, to see what I see!

(The **King** and **Polonius** enter.)

KING: His thoughts are not of love!
The way he spoke—it was not like madness.
There's something in his soul that sadness

Sits on, like a hen on eggs. When they hatch,
There will be some danger. To prevent it,
I have a plan. Hamlet will go to England.
The English king owes us some money,
And Hamlet can collect it.
Perhaps the seas, and different countries,
Will bring Hamlet back to himself.
What do you think of this idea, Polonius?

POLONIUS: It should work. But I do believe
That his grief springs from neglected love.
My lord, do as you please.
But may I suggest this:
After the play, let his mother meet with him
In private. Maybe she can get him to talk.
I'll hide in the room so I can overhear them.
If she can't uncover his grief, send him
To England—or lock him up wherever
You think would be best.

KING: It shall be so: Madness in great ones
Must not go unwatched.

(**All** exit.)

Scene ❷ 🎧

(**Hamlet** and **certain actors** enter a hall in the castle.)

ACT 3
SCENE 2

HAMLET: Say the speech as I pronounced it to you, trippingly on the tongue. If you yell it, as many of your actors do, I'd just as soon have the town-crier speak my lines. Do not saw the air too much with your hands, but use gentle motions. It is much better to act with a smoothness. Do not be too boring, either. Use your own judgment. Suit the action to the word, the word to the action. Remember that the purpose of acting is to hold the mirror up to nature. In other words, show things as they are. Now go and get ready.

(**Actors** exit. **Horatio** enters.)

HAMLET: Greetings, Horatio!

HORATIO: Sweet lord, I am at your service.

HAMLET: Horatio, you are as sensible a man
As I have ever known.

HORATIO: Oh, my dear lord—

HAMLET: I am not saying this to flatter you.

What advantage could I hope for from you?
You have no wealth but your good spirits to
Feed and clothe you. Why should anyone
Flatter the poor? Since I could distinguish
Among men, I chose you as a friend.
Even though you have had some bad luck,
You have never complained. You take the
Bad with the good, with equal thanks.
Blessed are those that can keep on going
No matter how fate treats them.
Give me the man who is not passion's slave,
And I will hold him in my heart—
As I do you! But enough of this.
There is a play tonight before the king.
One scene in it is very close to
What I have told you of my father's death.
When you see that act on stage,
Watch my uncle. If his hidden guilt
Does not make itself known at that point,
I'll be very surprised. I, too, will keep
My eyes on his face. After the play, we will
Compare notes about what we have seen.

HORATIO: Very well, my lord.

HAMLET: I hear them coming to the play.

I must start my mad act again.

Find yourself a place to sit.

(Trumpets are heard offstage, announcing the king and queen. **King**, **Queen**, **Polonius**, **Rosencrantz**, **Guildenstern**, and **others** enter.)

KING: How are you this evening, Hamlet?

HAMLET: Excellent, to be sure. Like a chameleon,

I eat the air, full of promises.

You cannot feed chickens that way.

KING: You make no sense, Hamlet.

HAMLET: Nor to me, either. Are the actors

ready?

ROSENCRANTZ: Yes, my lord.

QUEEN: Come here, my dear Hamlet, sit by me.

HAMLET: No, good mother. Something more

attractive pulls me.

POLONIUS *(to the king):* Did you hear that?

HAMLET *(to Ophelia):* Lady, shall I lie in your lap?

(He lies down at Ophelia's feet.)

OPHELIA *(blushing):* No, my lord!

HAMLET: I mean, my head upon your lap?

OPHELIA: Well, yes, my lord. You are in a merry mood, my lord.

HAMLET: Why shouldn't I be? Look how cheerful my mother looks—and my father has been dead less than two hours.

OPHELIA: No, it's been four months, my lord.

HAMLET: So long? Oh, heavens! Dead two months, and not forgotten yet? Then there's hope that a great man's memory may outlive his life by half a year!

(Trumpets are heard offstage. A **mime show** enters. The actor king and queen very lovingly embrace. He rests his head upon her shoulder, and she lays him down on a bed of flowers. Then, seeing that he is asleep, she leaves. A short time later, in comes another man. He takes off the king's crown, kisses it, pours poison in the king's ears, and exits. The queen returns, finds the king dead, and mourns loudly. The poisoner comes in again, with three or four others, seeming to mourn with her. The dead body is carried away. The poisoner woos the queen with gifts. For a while, she seems put off and unwilling, but in the end she accepts his love. All the **actors** exit.)

OPHELIA: What does this mean, my lord?

HAMLET: It means mischief.

(The **announcer** enters.)

ANNOUNCER: For us, and for our play,
  We hope you like what it does say,
  And now we'll start, with no delay.

OPHELIA: That was brief, my lord.

HAMLET: As brief as woman's love.

(**Actor King** and **Actor Queen** enter.)

ACTOR KING: It has been thirty years
  Since love united us in marriage.

ACTOR QUEEN: May it be thirty more
  Before our love is over!
  But, woe is me, you are so sick lately.
  As big as my love is, my fear is just as big.

ACTOR KING: Yes, I must leave you soon, love
  You shall live in this fair world after me.
  My honored and dear wife,
  I hope your next husband shall be as kind—

ACTOR QUEEN: Oh, stop talking like that!
  If I take a second husband, let me be cursed!
  For none wed the second
  But those who killed the first.

HAMLET *(aside):* Bitter thoughts!

ACTOR QUEEN: The only reason

For a second marriage is money, not love.
It would kill my husband a second time,
When the second husband kisses me.

ACTOR KING: I know you mean that now,
But later you might break that vow.
Nothing lasts forever, so it's not strange
That even our love might someday change.
You think you'd no second husband wed,
But that might change when the first is dead.

ACTOR QUEEN: Dear, I swear that this is true:
The only one I'll ever love is you.

ACTOR KING: What a deep vow!
Sweet, leave me now.
I must sleep. (He sleeps.)

ACTOR QUEEN: My dear, may sleep rest you,
And may nothing come between us two.
(**Actor Queen** exits.)

HAMLET *(to Queen):* How do you like it so far?

QUEEN: The lady protests too much, I think.

HAMLET: Oh, but she'll keep her word.

KING: Have you already seen this play?
Is there anything offensive in it?

HAMLET: No, no! They are just acting. The poison is not real. There's no offense in the world.

KING: What do you call the play?

HAMLET: "The Mousetrap." It's based on a murder done in Vienna. Gonzago is the duke's name. His wife is Baptista. You shall see. It's a play about evil, but what of it? Your majesty and all of us with clear consciences—it can't touch us.

(**First actor** enters.)

FIRST ACTOR: Evil thoughts, busy hands, strong poison, and no witnesses! It's perfect!

(He pours poison into the Actor King's ear.)

HAMLET: He poisons him in the garden for his money. The story is written in excellent Italian. Later you shall see how the murderer gets the love of Gonzago's wife.

(The king gets up.)

OPHELIA: The king rises.

HAMLET: Why? Did something frighten him?

QUEEN *(to King)*: What's wrong, my lord?

POLONIUS: Stop the play.

KING: Give me some light. Let's go!

ALL: Lights, lights, lights!

(**All** exit but Hamlet and Horatio.)

HAMLET: Horatio, did you watch him?

HORATIO: Very well, my lord.

HAMLET: During the talk about the poisoning?

HORATIO: I watched him very closely.

HAMLET: Ah, ha!

(**Rosencrantz** and **Guildenstern** enter.)

GUILDENSTERN: My lord, may I have a word?

HAMLET: Sir, you may have a whole story.

GUILDENSTERN: The king, sir. He is very upset.

HAMLET: Too much to drink, sir?

GUILDENSTERN: No, my lord. He seems quite ill.
The queen, your mother, has sent me.
She wants me to tell you that she is amazed
and astonished by your behavior.

HAMLET: Oh wonderful son, who can so astonish
a mother! Did she say anything else?

ROSENCRANTZ: She wants to speak with you in
her room before you go to bed.

HAMLET: I shall obey. Now, leave me, friends.

(**Rosencrantz**, **Guildenstern**, and **Horatio** exit.)

It is now the very witching time of night,
When evil comes out into the world.
Now I could drink hot blood and do
Such bitter business that the day would
Shake to look at it. Now to my mother—
Oh, heart, do not lose your nature.
Let me be cruel to her, not unnatural.
I will speak daggers to her, but use none.
After all, she is my mother. I am her son.

(**Hamlet** exits.)

Scene ❸ 🎧

(The **King**, **Rosencrantz**, and **Guildenstern** enter a room in the castle.)

KING: I don't like him, and I don't feel safe
　　　Around him when he is mad. Therefore,
　　　Prepare to go to England with him.

GUILDENSTERN: Yes, your majesty.
　　　It is our sacred duty to keep you safe,
　　　For so many people depend on you.

KING: Get ready for this speedy voyage.
　　　We will put chains around this fear
　　　Which now runs about so freely.

(**Rosencrantz** and **Guildenstern** exit. **Polonius** enters.)

POLONIUS: He's going to his mother's room.
　　　Behind the drapes I'll hide and listen.
　　　I'm sure she'll find out what's wrong.
　　　Before you go to bed I'll call on you
　　　And tell you what I know.

KING: Thanks, my dear sir.

(**Polonius** exits.)

Oh, my crime is terrible! It smells to heaven!
Like Cain in the Bible story, I have
Murdered my own brother! I cannot pray,
Though I want to so badly.
My stronger guilt defeats my strong desire.

Like a man with two things to do,
I stand here, wondering where to begin
And neglect both. This cursed hand seems
Thicker than itself with brother's blood.
Is there not rain enough in the heavens
To wash it white as snow? What prayer
Could I use? "Forgive me my foul murder"?
That cannot be, since I still have
All those things for which I did the murder:
My crown, my ambition, and my queen.
May one be pardoned and keep the goods?
In this evil world, money buys justice.
It can often buy the law, too. But it is not so
In heaven. No trickery there. What then?
What happens when one cannot repent?
Oh, wretched state! Oh, soul black as death!
Bow, stubborn knees! And, heart like steel,
Be soft as a newborn babe's skin!
All may be well.

(The King kneels. **Hamlet** enters.)

HAMLET *(aside)*: Now I could easily do it.

    (He draws his sword.) But, no!

    If I do it now, he goes to heaven.

    A villain kills my father, and for that,

    I, his only son, send the villain to heaven.

    Oh, this would be foolish, not revenge!

    He took my father by surprise,

    With all his crimes on his head, lusty as May.

    How his record stands, only heaven knows.

    No. Up, sword, and be ready later,

    When he is drunk, in his rage,

    Or in the evil pleasure of his bed.

    Gambling, or swearing, or doing something

    That does not lead to heaven. Then get him,

    So his heels may kick at heaven and his soul

    May go to hell, where it belongs.

(**Hamlet** exits. The King rises.)

KING: My words fly up,

    But my thoughts remain below.

    Words without thoughts never to heaven go.

(The **King** exits.)

Scene 4

(The **Queen** and **Polonius** enter her room.)

POLONIUS: He is on his way. Now, be firm.
Tell him his pranks have been out of hand.
Say that you have spared him trouble until now.
I'll hide here silently.

HAMLET *(from offstage):* Mother, Mother!

QUEEN: Hide! I hear him coming.

(Polonius hides behind the drapes. **Hamlet** enters.)

HAMLET: Now, Mother, what's the matter?

QUEEN *(referring to King Claudius):* Hamlet, you
have offended your father.

HAMLET *(referring to the dead King Hamlet):*
Mother, you have offended my father.

QUEEN: Come, come, you answer with an idle
tongue.

HAMLET: Go, go, you question with a wicked tongue!

QUEEN: Have you forgotten who I am?

HAMLET: Of course not. You are the queen,
Your husband's brother's wife, and—
I wish it were not so—you are my mother.

73

QUEEN: Don't speak to me like that!

HAMLET: Come, come, sit down. Do not move.
Sit here until I set up a mirror where you
May see the innermost part of yourself.

QUEEN: What will you do? Murder me?
Help, help!

POLONIUS *(from behind the drapes)*: Help!

HAMLET *(drawing his sword)*: What's that—a rat?

(He stabs through the drapes.)

POLONIUS: Oh, I am killed! (Polonius dies.)

QUEEN: Oh, my, what have you done?

HAMLET: I don't know. Is it the king?

(Hamlet draws forth Polonius.)

QUEEN: Oh, what a rash and bloody deed!

HAMLET: Almost as bad, good Mother,
As killing a king and marrying his brother

QUEEN: Killing a king?

HAMLET: Yes, lady, that's what I said.
(to Polonius): You wretched fool, farewell!
I thought you were the king. You found out
That being too busy is dangerous.

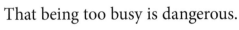

(to the queen): Stop wringing your hands.
Sit down, and let me wring your heart.
For so I shall, unless it has become too hard.

QUEEN: What have I done, that you dare
Wag your tongue so rudely against me?

HAMLET: An act that takes the rose
From the fair forehead of an innocent love
And sets a blister there. An act that makes
Marriage vows as false as gamblers' oaths.
All of heaven is sick from thinking about it.

QUEEN: What act? What do you mean?

HAMLET: Think about your husband, so good
That he was almost like a god.
Now look at your present husband.
Do you have eyes?
You cannot call it love, for at your age,
The passion in the blood is tame.
Who would go from my father to his
   own brother?
What devil fooled you into doing it?
Oh, shame! Where is your blush?

QUEEN: Oh, Hamlet, speak no more.
You turn my eyes into my very soul.
There I see such black and grained spots
That will never come clean.
I beg you, say no more!
These words are like daggers in my ears.
No more, sweet Hamlet.

HAMLET: He is a murderer and a villain,
A wretch not worth a twentieth of a tenth
Of your former husband. A monster who
Stole the crown and put it in his pocket!

QUEEN: No more!

HAMLET: A king of rags and patches!

(The **Ghost** enters, visible only to Hamlet.)

Save me and hover over me, you angels!
(to the Ghost): What is it, your grace?

QUEEN: Oh, no, he's mad!

HAMLET: Have you come to scold your son
Who has not yet taken revenge? Tell me!

GHOST: Do not forget. This visit
Is meant to push you a little.
But, look at your mother. She suffers.
Step between her and her fighting soul.
Speak to her, Hamlet.

HAMLET: How is it with you, lady?

QUEEN: No, how is it with you?
You look at nothing and speak to the air?
What are you looking at?

HAMLET: At him, at him! See how pale he is!

QUEEN: Dear son, nothing is there.

HAMLET: Do you see nothing there?

QUEEN: Nothing at all.

HAMLET: Did you hear nothing?

QUEEN: No, nothing but ourselves.

HAMLET: Why, look there!

See how it steals away!

My father, dressed as when he was alive.

Look—he is going out the door now!

(The **Ghost** exits.)

QUEEN: You are seeing things that don't exist.

HAMLET: Mother, confess your sins to heaven.

Repent what's past. Avoid what is to come.

QUEEN: Son, you have broken my heart in two.

HAMLET: Then throw away the worse part

And live more purely with the other half.

Good night. But do not go to my uncle's bed

Pretend to be good, even if you are not.

Stay away tonight, and that

Will make it easier tomorrow night

The next night, it will be even easier.

(pointing to Polonius): For this, I am sorry,

But it has pleased heaven

To punish me with this, and this with me.

I will answer for the death I gave him.

So again, good night.

I must be cruel, only to be kind—

Thus bad begins, and worse remains behind.

But one more thing, good lady . . .

QUEEN: What is it?

HAMLET: I must go to England. Did you know?

QUEEN: I had forgotten. But, yes, you are right.

HAMLET: My two friends—whom I trust as I
Trust poisonous snakes—will go with me
To deliver sealed letters from the king.
So be it. It's fun to see the hangman hanged
With his own noose. I know the plan,
And they won't be able to get the best of me.
(pointing to Polonius): I'll drag the body out.
Indeed, this adviser is now so still, so grave,
Who was in life a foolish old knave.
Good night, Mother.

(**All** exit, Hamlet dragging out Polonius.)

ACT 4

Summary

國王發現他是哈姆雷特欲復仇的對象,便派哈姆雷特去英格蘭。他還寫信給英格蘭國王,要求他在哈姆雷特抵達時就處死他。哈姆雷特聽聞福丁布拉正揮軍波蘭,很欣賞他的勇氣,並認為自己膽怯怕死。他再度立下將為亡父復仇的誓言。

歐菲莉亞去造訪皇后且舉止瘋癲。當雷爾提回到丹麥時,他因妹妹不幸的狀態而備感憂傷。當哈姆雷特的船隻被海盜攻擊後,他給予海盜獎賞請他們帶他回丹麥。國王與雷爾提打算在劍術比賽中了結哈姆雷特的性命,在他們商議之時,皇后上場並告知歐菲莉亞溺斃的消息。

Scene ❶ 🎧

(The **King** enters a room in the castle, joining the Queen, who is groaning.)

KING: These sighs must mean something.

QUEEN: Oh, what I have seen tonight!

KING: What, Gertrude? How is Hamlet?

QUEEN: Mad as the wind in a storm.
    He heard a noise from behind the drapes,
    Cried out, "A rat," and killed Polonius!

KING: Oh, heavy deed!
    It would have been my fate, if I'd been there.
    How will we explain this bloody deed?
    The people will blame us. Where is he?

QUEEN: He has taken away the body.

KING: Oh, Gertrude, we have to find him.
    We'll put him on a ship right away.
    This vile deed must somehow be explained.

(**Rosencrantz** and **Guildenstern** enter.)

    Greetings, friends. We need some help.
    In his madness, Hamlet has killed Polonius
    And dragged the body away.

Go find him, and bring the body
Into the chapel. I beg you, hurry!

(**Rosencrantz** and **Guildenstern** exit.)

Gertrude, we'll talk to our wisest friends.
We'll let them know what has happened
And what we plan to do. Perhaps then they
Won't blame us for it. Oh, come away!
My soul is full of pain and dismay.

(**King** and **Queen** exit.)

Scene ❷ (15)

(**Hamlet** enters another room in the castle.)

HAMLET: The body is safely hidden.

ROSENCRANTZ AND GUILDENSTERN *(from offstage)*:
Hamlet! Lord Hamlet!

HAMLET: Who's calling me? Here they come.

(**Rosencrantz** and **Guildenstern** enter.)

ROSENCRANTZ: Sir, where is the body?

HAMLET: I've mixed it with the dust.

ROSENCRANTZ: Tell us where it is, so we may
take it to the chapel.

HAMLET: Why should I be spoken to like this
by a sponge like you?

ROSENCRANTZ: You take me for a sponge?

HAMLET: Yes, one that soaks up the king's favor
and rewards. When he wants to find out
what you know, all he has to do is squeeze
you. Then, sponge, you become dry again.

ROSENCRANTZ: I do not understand you, lord.

HAMLET: I am not surprised. A good speech means

nothing to a foolish ear. Take me to the king.

(**All** exit.)

Scene 3 (16)

(**King**, with **attendants**, enters another room.)

KING: I have sent them to look for Hamlet And to find the body. Hamlet is dangerous! Yet we must not bring the law upon him. He is loved by the people. To keep peace, His sudden leaving must seem planned.

(**Rosencrantz**, **Guildenstern**, and **Hamlet** enter.)

Now, Hamlet, where's Polonius?

HAMLET: At supper.

KING: At supper! Where?

HAMLET: Not where he eats,

But where the worms are eating him.

KING: Now, now. Tell us where Polonius is.

HAMLET: In heaven. Send for him there. If your messenger doesn't find him, Seek him in the other place yourself.

But if you don't find him this month,

You shall smell him as you go into the lobby.

KING (*to attendants*): Go seek him there.

HAMLET: He will stay there until you come.

(**Attendants** exit.)

KING: Hamlet, for your own safety, we must
    Send you away with fiery quickness.
    So get ready. The ship is waiting, and
    The wind is high. You must go to England.

HAMLET: Good. Farewell, dear Mother.

KING: I am your loving father, Hamlet.

HAMLET: You are my mother.
    Father and mother are man and wife.
    Man and wife are one flesh.
    And so, you are my mother.
    Now, on to England!

(**Hamlet** exits.)

KING *(to Rosencrantz and Guildenstern)*: Follow him.
    Make him hurry. Do not delay.
    I want him out of here tonight. Away!
    Everything is ready. Make haste!

(**All** exit but the King.)

    King of England, if you value my good will,
    You'll do what I ask in the letter. I want
    The immediate death of Hamlet.

He rages in my blood like a sickness,
And you must cure me! Until I know it's done,
Whatever my luck, my joy will not be won.

(**King** exits.)

ACT 4
SCENE 3

Scene ④ 🎧

(**Fortinbras** enters, leading marching forces across a plain in Denmark.)

FORTINBRAS *(to Captain)*: Go and greet
  The Danish king. Find out if he will
  Still allow us to march across his land
  On our way to Poland.

CAPTAIN: Yes, my lord.

(**All** but the Captain exit. **Hamlet**, **Rosencrantz**, and **Guildenstern** enter.)

HAMLET: Good sir, whose army is that?
  Who commands it, and why is it here?

CAPTAIN: It is Norway's army, sir,
  Commanded by Fortinbras, the nephew
  Of the King of Norway. He is on his way
  To fight against some part of Poland.
  We go to gain a little patch of ground
  That is worth very little.

HAMLET: Why, then, the Polish king
  Won't even defend it.

CAPTAIN: On the contrary, sir.

The Polish army is already there.

HAMLET: What a waste! Thousands of men
  Will die for no reason. I thank you, sir.

CAPTAIN: God be with you, sir.

(**Captain** exits.)

ROSENCRANTZ: Are you ready to go, my lord?

HAMLET: I'll be right with you. Go on ahead.

(**All** exit but Hamlet.)

ACT 4
SCENE 4

  How everything pushes me on to revenge!
  What is a man, if all he does is eat and sleep?
  A beast, no more. Surely he who made us
  Able to think and reason
  Meant for us to use that ability.
  Now, perhaps I think too much.
  Maybe I am one part wisdom and
  Three parts coward. I do not know
  Why I say "I must do this thing,"
  Unless I have the cause, the will,
  The strength, and the means to do it.
  The examples of others urge me on.
  Look at this army, led by a tender prince.
  They will risk their lives for everything,

Even for an eggshell. At least Fortinbras
Acts to avenge his father. How about me,
Then, with a father killed, a mother stained?
To my shame, I see the approaching death
Of 20,000 men. They will fight for land
Not big enough for their graves.
Oh, from this time until the end,
May all my thoughts be for revenge!

(**Hamlet** exits.)

Scene ❺ 🎧 18

(The **Queen** and **Horatio** enter a room.)

QUEEN: What does Ophelia want?

HORATIO: She speaks of her father.
Her words don't make any sense.

QUEEN: Let her come in.

(**Horatio** exits.)

To my sick soul, everything seems
To suggest that danger is ahead.
So full of crippling fear is guilt,
It spills itself in fearing to be spilt!

(**Horatio** enters again, with **Ophelia**.)

OPHELIA: Where is the beautiful queen?

QUEEN: How are you, Ophelia?

OPHELIA *(singing):* "He is dead and gone, lady,
He is dead and gone.
At his head is green grass,
At his feet, a stone."

QUEEN: But Ophelia—

(The **King** enters.)

OPHELIA: Listen to this: *(singing)*:

> "His shroud is white as the mountain snow.
>
> He lies among sweet white flowers,
>
> Watered by our tearful showers."

KING: How are you, pretty lady?

QUEEN: She's obsessed with her father.

OPHELIA *(singing)*: "Tomorrow is

> Saint Valentine's day
>
> All in the morning time,
>
> And I a maid at your window,
>
> I'll be your Valentine.
>
> Then up he rose, put on his clothes,
>
> And opened the bedroom door.

Let in the maid, who stayed a while,
And was a maiden nevermore.
She said, 'Before you asked me in,
You promised we would wed.'
He said, 'It's true, I would have done it,
If you'd not come to my bed.'"

KING: How long has she been this way?

OPHELIA: I hope all will be well,
But I can't help crying.
To think they would lay him
In the cold, cold ground!
My brother shall hear of it.
And so I thank you for your good advice.
Come, my coach! Good night, sweet ladies.
Good night, ladies. Good night, good night!

(**Ophelia** exits.)

KING *(to Horatio)*: Follow her, will you?

(**Horatio** exits.)

Oh, this poison of deep grief springs
From her father's death. Oh, Gertrude,
When sorrows come, they do not come
As single spies, but as armies!

First, her father is killed.
Next, your son is gone. The people are upset
By talk of Polonius's death.
They think I had something to do with it.
Poor Ophelia! Divided from her own mind.
Laertes has secretly come back from France.
He has heard rumors about his father's
death. (He hears a noise from offstage.)
What's that? Where are my guards?

(A **gentleman** enters.)

GENTLEMAN: Save yourself, my lord:
Young Laertes and his rebel force
Have swept aside your own soldiers.
The mob calls him "Lord." They say,
"We have chosen! Laertes shall be king!"

(Noise is heard from offstage.)

KING: The doors are broken down!

(**Laertes** enters, followed by **some Danes**. The **gentleman** exits.)

LAERTES: Where is the king?
(to his followers): Guard the door.

DANES: We will, we will.

(The **Danes** exit.)

LAERTES *(to the king)*: Oh, you vile king,
　　Give me my father!

QUEEN: Calm down, good Laertes.

LAERTES: If one drop of my blood stays calm,
　　It would betray my father.

KING: Why are you so angry? Tell me!

LAERTES: Where is my father?

KING: Dead.

LAERTES: I will have revenge for my father's death!

KING: Good Laertes, in getting your revenge,
　　Will you kill both friend and foe?

LAERTES: None but his enemies.

KING: Do you wish to know who they are?

LAERTES: Of course.

KING: I had nothing to do with his death.
    I am in grief for it.

DANES *(from offstage):* Let her come in.

LAERTES: What noise is that?

(**Ophelia** enters again, wearing straw and flowers on her clothing and in her hair.)

    Ophelia! Oh, heat, dry up my brains!
    May salty tears burn out my eyes!
    By heaven, your madness shall be avenged!
    Dear maid, kind sister, sweet Ophelia!
    Oh, heavens! Can a young maid's wits
    Be as mortal as an old man's life?

OPHELIA *(singing):* "There, at his grave—
    Hey non nonny, hey nonny—
    Our tears we gave—"

LAERTES: If you were still sane, you could not
    Speak better for revenge.

OPHELIA *(singing):* "Will he come again?
    No, no, he is dead,

Go to your death bed,

He never will come again.

His beard was as white as snow,

He is gone, he is gone,

And all we can do is moan—

God have mercy on his soul!" (**She** exits.)

KING: Laertes, I share your grief.

Go now and find your wisest friends.

They shall listen to both of us and judge.

If they find me guilty, then you shall have

My kingdom, my crown, my life—

And all else that I call mine. If not,

Be patient, and we shall find a way

To make up for your loss.

ACT 4
SCENE 5

LAERTES: Let this be so.

The way he died, his secret burial—

No noble rites or formal ceremony—

All these things cry out for explanation.

KING: And you shall have it.

Where the guilt is, let the great axe fall.

Now, go with me.

(**All** exit.)

Scene 6 🎧19

(**Horatio** enters another room with a **servant**.)

HORATIO: Who wants to speak with me?

SERVANT: Sailors, sir, with letters for you.

HORATIO: Let them come in.

(**Servant** exits. **Sailors** enter.)

FIRST SAILOR: Greetings, sir. This letter comes from the ambassador who was on his way to England.

HORATIO *(reading):* "Dear Horatio,
When you have finished reading this, arrange for these fellows to see the king. They have some letters for him. Pirates boarded our ship two days after we set sail. In the battle that followed, I boarded their ship. As soon as they got clear of our ship, I alone became their prisoner. I have been treated well. They expect a favor from me in return. Let the king have the letters I have sent. Then come to me as fast as you would run

away from death. I have something to tell
you that will make you speechless. I do
not want to put it in writing. These good
fellows will bring you where I am.
Rosencrantz and Guildenstern are still on
their way to England. I have much to tell
you about them. Yours, Hamlet."
(to sailors): Come with me to the king.
Then you can take me to Hamlet.

(**All** exit.)

Scene 7 🎧 20

(The **King** and **Laertes** enter another room in the castle.)

KING: Now you know the whole story.

After Hamlet killed your father,

He tried to kill me.

LAERTES: It appears to be true. But tell me why

You did not punish him for these crimes.

KING: For two special reasons. The queen,

His mother, lives almost for his looks.

And I love her too much to let her be hurt.

Also, the common people love him.

No matter what I said about him,

They would never have believed it.

Their anger would have turned on me.

LAERTES *(bitterly)*: And so I have lost a noble father and

My sister has been driven to madness.

But my revenge will come!

KING: Do not lose sleep over it. Do not think

That I am ready to forget what happened.

You shall soon hear more.

I loved your father, and I love myself.

I will have my revenge for Hamlet's crimes!

(A **messenger** enters.)

MESSENGER: Letters, my lord, from Hamlet.

This one is for you. This is for the queen.

KING: From Hamlet! Who brought them?

MESSENGER: Sailors, my lord.

(**Messenger** exits.)

KING: Laertes, you shall hear this.

(reading): "Your majesty, I am back in your kingdom. Tomorrow I would like to see you and tell you the reasons for my sudden and strange return. Hamlet." What does this mean? Have the others come back, too?

LAERTES: Is it Hamlet's handwriting?

KING: Yes. What does it mean?

LAERTES: I have no idea, my lord.

But let him come.

It warms the sickness in my heart

That I shall have my revenge so soon.

KING: Will you take my advice, Laertes?

LAERTES: Yes, my lord—as long as you
Do not advise me to let Hamlet live.

KING: I have a plan for his death.
Even his mother will call it an accident.

LAERTES: My lord, I want a hand in it!

KING: I have heard that you are good at fencing.
They say you shine at the sport. In fact,
Hamlet is jealous of your reputation and
Would like nothing more than to beat you.

Now let me ask you a question.

What would you most like to do to Hamlet

To show that you are your father's son?

LAERTES: To cut his throat in the church!

KING: Revenge could take place anywhere.

But, good Laertes, here's a better plan:

Hamlet will be told that you are here.

We'll have some men praise your skill

At fencing and make bets on who would win

In a duel—you or Hamlet. He, unsuspecting,

Will not check the tips of the swords.

It would be easy for you to choose a sword

Whose tip was not covered for safety.

Then, in one practice pass,

You can settle with him for your father.

LAERTES: I will do it!

And to make sure, I'll put some poison

On the tip of my sword. I have it already.

It is so strong that there is no antidote.

KING: Let's think some more about this.

If our plan fails, it would make us look bad.

It would be better not to try than to fail.

That is why we should have a backup plan.

MLet me see . . . Ah! I have it!

As you duel, you'll both get thirsty.

When he calls for drink, I'll have prepared

A cup for him. If he by chance escapes

The poison on your sword,

He'll get it from the cup.

(The **Queen** enters, greatly upset.)

QUEEN: One sorrow after another—

Your sister's drowned, Laertes.

LAERTES: Drowned! Oh, where?

QUEEN: There is a willow tree by the brook.

Its leaves reflect in the glassy stream.

While making flower chains there, she

Climbed up on an overhanging tree branch

To hang her garlands from it.

The branch broke off, and she fell into the

Weeping brook. For a while, her clothes
   spread wide

And held her up like a mermaid.

But then, heavy with water, her clothes

Pulled the poor wretch to muddy death.

LAERTES: Alas, then she is drowned?

AMLET

QUEEN: Drowned, drowned . . .

LAERTES: You've had too much water,
Poor Ophelia, so I'll hold back my tears.
But I'm only human. I cannot. (**He** cries.)
When these tears are gone, that will be
The last of the woman in me. (**He** exits.)

KING: Let us follow him, Gertrude.
It took all I had to calm his rage!
This sad news is sure to revive it.
Therefore, let us follow him.

(The **King** and **Queen** exit.)

ACT 5

Summary

有兩位掘墓人正在替歐菲莉亞掘墓,哈姆雷特對赫瑞修訴說死亡對於眾人一視同仁的道理。在歐菲莉亞的葬禮上,哈姆雷特和雷爾提爭論誰較愛歐菲莉亞。隨後,哈姆雷特表示他將國王的信函與自己寫的調換,當羅生克蘭和蓋登思鄧將信函交給英格蘭王時,他們將會被立即處死,而非哈姆雷特。

哈姆雷特和雷爾提進行先前計畫好的劍術決鬥,結果造成哈姆雷特、雷爾提、國王和皇后之死。小福丁布拉從波蘭凱旋歸來,並宣誓成為丹麥的新國王。

Scene ❶ 🎧

(A **gravedigger** and his **helper** enter a churchyard.)

GRAVEDIGGER: Is she to have a Christian burial
Even though she was a suicide?

HELPER: That's what I heard.

GRAVEDIGGER: How can that be?
Did she drown herself in self-defense?

HELPER: The coroner said it wasn't suicide.
Maybe she's getting the benefit of the doubt
Because she was a gentlewoman.

GRAVEDIGGER: Who knows? And who cares?
All I want is a drink. Why don't you go
And get us something at the tavern?

(**Helper** exits. **Hamlet** and **Horatio** enter, and stand at
a distance. They watch as the gravedigger digs and sings.)

HAMLET: Has he no feeling for his work?
How can he sing while he digs a grave?

HORATIO: He is so used to digging graves
That he doesn't really think about it.

HAMLET: You're probably right.
Only those who don't work very hard

Have time for dainty feelings.

GRAVEDIGGER (*singing*): "A pickaxe
And a spade, a spade,
Dig a deep pit for the latest guest.
Bring a burial sheet for the lovely maid
Who will soon be here for her final rest."

(He hits a skull with his shovel and throws it up to the surface.)

HAMLET: There's a skull. Could it be
The skull of a lawyer?
Where are his arguments now, his cases,
His evidence, and his tricks? Why does he let
This rude man now knock him about
With a dirty shovel? Shouldn't he accuse
The brute of assault? Hmmm. This fellow
Might have been a great buyer of land.
Is this how he ends up—
With his fine head full of fine dirt?
All his deeds and legal papers would
Just about fit in this box. Must the buyer
Himself have no more room than this?

 HORATIO: Not an inch more, my lord.

HAMLET: I will speak to this fellow.

(to the gravedigger): Whose grave is this?

GRAVEDIGGER: Mine, sir.

HAMLET: What man do you dig it for?

GRAVEDIGGER: For no man, sir.

HAMLET: What woman, then? 81

GRAVEDIGGER: For no woman, either.

HAMLET: Who is to be buried in it?

GRAVEDIGGER: One who was a woman, sir.
But, rest her soul, she's dead.

HAMLET: How careful you are with words!
How long have you been a gravedigger?

GRAVEDIGGER: I began on the day that our

Last King Hamlet defeated old Fortinbras,
Thirty years ago. It was the very day
That young Hamlet was born—
He that has been sent to England.

HAMLET: Why was he sent to England?

GRAVEDIGGER: Why, because he is mad.
He shall recover his wits there.
Or, if he does not, it won't matter much.

HAMLET: Why?

ACT 5
SCENE
1

GRAVEDIGGER: No one in England will notice. There, all the men are as mad as he.

HAMLET: Say, how long will a man lie in the earth before he rots?

GRAVEDIGGER: Eight or nine years. (He picks up a skull.) Here's a skull now. This skull has been in the earth for twenty-three years.

HAMLET: Whose was it?

GRAVEDIGGER: This, sir, was Yorick's skull— the king's jester.

HAMLET: Let me see. (He takes the skull.)

Alas, poor Yorick! I knew him, Horatio.
He was a fellow of infinite fun.
He carried me on his back 1,000 times.
I hate to think of this!
Where are your jokes now, your tricks,
Your songs, your flashes of merriment?
Not one is left to mock your grinning?
Go to my lady's room right now.
Tell her that no matter how thick she puts
On her makeup, she will end up like this.
Make her laugh at that.
Horatio, do you think Alexander the Great
Looked like this in the earth?

HORATIO: Just the same.

HAMLET: And smelled like this? Pah!

(He throws down the skull.)

HORATIO: Just the same, my lord.

HAMLET: To what lowly uses we may return,
Horatio! Even the noble dust of Alexander
Might end up stopping up a knot-hole.

HORATIO: You think too much, Hamlet.

HAMLET: But just consider it for a minute:

Alexander died, Alexander was buried,

Alexander returned to dust. The dust is earth.

From earth we get clay. That very clay

Might someday stop a hole in a beer-barrel.

The imperial Caesar, dead and turned to clay,

Might stop a hole to keep the wind away.

Oh, that he who awed the world might

Patch a wall to keep the winter wind out!

But, that's enough for now. Look!

Here comes the king.

(**Priests** enter, leading a procession. The **King**, the **Queen**, **Laertes**, and **mourners** follow. **Attendants** carry a coffin.)

Who could be in the coffin?

The queen is here, but so few mourners!

This suggests a suicide. It must have been

Someone of high rank. Let's hide and watch.

(**Hamlet** and **Horatio** hide.)

LAERTES: What other ceremonies will there be?

FIRST PRIEST: We have already done all we can

For her funeral. Her death was doubtful.

She should be buried in unblessed ground,

And pebbles thrown on her.

Yet here she is allowed her virgin rites,

With flowers and prayers and funeral bells.

LAERTES *(sadly)*: Can no more be done?

FIRST PRIEST: No more may be done.

We would mock the service of the dead

To give her the same respect we show

To souls who parted in peace.

LAERTES: Lay her in the earth.

From her fair and pure flesh

May violets spring! I tell you, selfish priest,

My sister will be an angel

When you lie howling below.

HAMLET: What—it's the fair Ophelia?

QUEEN *(scattering flowers)*: Sweets to the sweet.

Farewell. I hoped that you would marry
    Hamlet.

I wanted to scatter flowers on

Your bridal bed, sweet maid.

Instead, I put them on your grave.

LAERTES: Oh, may countless woes fall on

The man who caused her madness!

Don't bury her until I have held her
Once more in my arms! (He leaps into the grave.)
Now pile your dust on both of us!

HAMLET *(advancing)*: Who is this
Who makes such a show of his grief?

LAERTES: Who is this who comes uninvited?

HAMLET *(leaping into the grave)*: It is I, Hamlet
the Dane.

LAERTES *(fighting with him)*: Her death
Was all your fault, you monster!

HAMLET: You are wrong about that.
Take your fingers from my throat!

KING *(to some attendants)*: Pull them apart!

QUEEN: Hamlet! Hamlet!

(Attendants part them. They come out of the grave.)

HAMLET: Why, I will fight him about this
Until the last moment of my life!

QUEEN: Oh, my son, about what?

HAMLET: I loved Ophelia! Not even 40,000
brothers, with all their love,
Could love her as much.

KING: Oh, he is mad, Laertes!

QUEEN: For the sake of God, leave him alone!

HAMLET *(to Laertes)*: Did you come to whine?
   To show your love by leaping into her grave?
   Be buried alive with her, and so will I.
   If you're going to rant and rave,
   I'll rant as well as you!

QUEEN: This is madness.

HAMLET: Laertes, why do you accuse me?
   I have always loved you like a brother.
   But it doesn't matter.
   You may do what you may.
   The cat will mew, the dog will have his day.

(**Hamlet** exits.)

KING: Good Horatio, look after him.

(**Horatio** exits.)

   (to Laertes): Be patient. Think about our talk
      last night.
   You'll soon have another chance to fight.

(**All** exit.)

Scene ❷ 🎧

(**Hamlet** and **Horatio** enter a hall in the castle.)

HAMLET: In my letter, I mentioned that I
    Wanted to tell you some things in person.
    We were on our way to England—
    Rosencrantz, Guildenstern, and I.
    In my heart there was a kind of fighting
    That kept me awake. On an impulse—
    And praise be to heaven for such impulses—
    I got up from my bunk and left my cabin.
    I wrapped my sailor's coat around me
    And groped around in the dark to find them.
    I finally found them asleep, and I stole
    Their packet of letters. I went back
    To my own room again, my fears forgetting
    My manners. I opened their letters.
    There I found—oh, royal treachery!—
    A message from our king
    To the King of England. It said that,
    Upon opening the letter, without even
    Taking time to sharpen the axe, the king
    Was to have my head cut off!

HORATIO *(shocked)*: Is it possible?

HAMLET: Here's the letter—read it yourself.

But do you want to know what I did next?

HORATIO: I beg you.

HAMLET: I sat down and wrote a new letter.

In it, I mentioned how the King of England
And the King of Denmark have always been
Good friends. In the name of the friendship,
I said that, without stopping to debate,
He should put the bearers of the letter
To sudden death. They were not to be given
Any time to say their prayers.
Naturally, I signed it with the name of my

Mother's husband. I had my father's
Official sealing ring in my bag.
It matches the present king's seal.
I folded the letter like the other.
I sealed it with wax and placed it safely
Back where I had found the first one
Rosencrantz and Guildenstern never
Knew about the change. Now, the next day
Was our sea-fight, when the pirates attacked.
What happened after that, you already know.

HORATIO: So Guildenstern and Rosencrantz
Went to their deaths?

HAMLET: Why, man, they loved their work!
They are not on my conscience.
Their defeat was their own fault.
When lesser men come between the swords
Of the mighty, they take their own risks.

HORATIO: What kind of a king do we have?

HAMLET: He killed my father,
Disgraced my mother, and
Stood between me and the crown.
Then he tried to have me killed!

Wouldn't it be perfect if I could put an end
To him with my own hands?

HORATIO: He will soon learn what happened
When the King of England got your letter.

HAMLET: Yes, but meanwhile, the time is mine.
It doesn't take long to end a man's life.
But I am very sorry, good Horatio,
That I lost control of myself with Laertes.
I'll try to make it up to him. But, still,
His grief made mine even greater.

HORATIO: Quiet! Someone's coming.

ACT 5
SCENE 2

(**Osric** enters.)

OSRIC: My lord, welcome back to Denmark.

HAMLET: I humbly thank you, sir.

OSRIC: Sir, his majesty asked me to tell you
That he has placed a large bet on your skill.
As you may already know, Laertes
Is a highly skilled swordsman.
It is said that no one is better than he.
The king, sir, has bet six fine horses
That you can beat Laertes in a duel.
The exact bet is this: In 12 passes,

Laertes shall not hit you more than 3 times.
Laertes, on the other hand, has said that
He will hit you 9 times out of 12.
The bet could be settled immediately
If your lordship would accept the challenge.

HAMLET: I am willing. I will win for the king
If I can. If not, I will gain nothing
But my shame and the odd hits.

OSRIC: My lord, I shall deliver your message.

(**Osric** exits.)

HORATIO: You will lose this wager, my lord.

HAMLET: I do not think so. Since Laertes went to
France, I have been practicing. I shall win
with those odds. Don't think I'm not a
little nervous about it. But it doesn't matter.

HORATIO (*worried*)**:** If you have any bad feelings
about this, I will say that you are ill.

HAMLET: Not at all. I don't pay attention to
omens and bad feelings. There is a special
plan in the death of a sparrow. If death
comes now, it won't come later. If it is
not to come later, it will come now. In

any case, it will come sooner or later.

Being ready for it is all that matters.

(The **King**, the **Queen**, **Laertes**, **lords**, **Osric**, and **attendants** carrying swords enter.)

KING: Hamlet, shake hands with Laertes.

(The king puts Laertes's hand into Hamlet's.)

HAMLET *(to Laertes):* Give me your pardon, sir.

I have done you wrong. You must have heard

That I am not myself lately.

Forgive me if I offended you.

LAERTES: I accept your apology.

KING: Give them the swords, young Osric.

Hamlet, you know the wager?

HAMLET: Very well, my lord.

Your grace has bet on the weaker side.

KING: I do not think so. I have seen you both.

I think you will give Laertes a good fight.

LAERTES *(seeing that he has not been given the poisoned sword)*: This one is too heavy.

Let me see another.

HAMLET: This one is fine for me!

(They prepare to duel. **Servants** enter with cups of wine.)

KING: Set the cups of wine upon that table.

If Hamlet wins, I'll drink to his health!

(They begin. Hamlet scores the first point.)

KING: I'll drink to that! Your health, Hamlet.

(He drinks some wine. Then, as trumpets play, he secretly puts the poison into another cup of wine and raises it, offering it to Hamlet.)

Have a sip yourself.

HAMLET: I'll play this bout first. Set it down for a while. *(to Laertes)*: Come on.

(They play, and Hamlet scores again.)

KING *(to the queen)*: Our son shall win.

QUEEN: But he's out of shape and short of breath. *(to Hamlet)*: Hamlet, take my napkin, wipe your forehead. *(picking up the poisoned cup that the king has set aside for Hamlet)*: I'll drink to your good luck, Hamlet.

KING: Gertrude, do not drink!

QUEEN: I shall, my lord, if you don't mind.

(She drinks and offers the cup to Hamlet.)

KING *(aside)*: The poisoned cup! It is too late.

HAMLET *(to the queen)*: Not yet, thanks. Later.

(They continue their swordplay. Fighting fiercely, Laertes wounds Hamlet with the poisoned sword. As they fight on, they drop their swords during a scuffle. Each one accidentally picks up the other's sword. Then Hamlet wounds Laertes with the poisoned sword—just as the queen falls.)

HORATIO: Both of them are bleeding!
(to Hamlet): How are you, my lord?

OSRIC *(to Laertes)*: How are you, Laertes?

LAERTES: Why, as a bird

Caught in my own trap, Osric.

I am justly killed by my own treachery.

HAMLET: How is the queen?

KING: She faints from seeing you bleed.

QUEEN: No, no! The drink, the drink!

Oh, my dear Hamlet! I am poisoned.

(The queen dies.)

HAMLET: Oh, villainy! Stop everything!

Let the door be locked! Find the traitor!

(Laertes falls.)

LAERTES: The traitor is here, Hamlet.

Hamlet, you are killed.

No medicine in the world can do you good.

In you there is not half an hour of life.

The treacherous weapon is in your hand.

The tip had no guard, and it was poisoned.

Both of us have been wounded by it.

Here I lie, never to rise again.

Your mother's poisoned.

I can say no more.

The king—the king's to blame.

HAMLET: The point is poisoned?

Then, poison, do your work!

(Hamlet stabs the king.)

OSRIC AND LORDS: Treason! Treason!

HAMLET: Here, you villain! Finish this!

Follow my mother!

(Hamlet forces the king to drink. The king dies.)

LAERTES: It is only fair. It was all his idea.

Exchange forgiveness with me, Hamlet.

I forgive you for my death and my father's.

Forgive me for yours. (Laertes dies.)

HAMLET: May heaven make you free of it!

I follow you. Unhappy queen, farewell!

I am dead, Horatio. You are alive.

Tell my story to those who don't know it.

HORATIO: Don't believe that I shall live.

There's still some wine left.

HAMLET: As you are a man, give me the cup.

Let it go, by heaven, I'll have it.

(Hamlet takes the cup from Horatio.)

Oh, good Horatio,

If you ever did hold me in your heart,

Stay away from happiness for a while,
And in this harsh world
Draw your breath in pain to tell my story.

(Marching and the sound of shots are heard.)

What warlike noise is that?

OSRIC: Young Fortinbras has returned in
victory from Poland. And the
ambassadors from England have also
come with news.

HAMLET: Oh, I die, Horatio!
I cannot live to hear the news from England.
But I predict that Fortinbras will be the next
King of Denmark. He has my dying vote.
Tell him— (He cannot finish the sentence.
The rest is silence. Hamlet dies.)

HORATIO: There ends a noble life.
Good night, sweet prince,
May flights of angels sing you to your rest!

(**Fortinbras**, **ambassadors**, and **others** enter.)

FORTINBRAS: What is all this?

HORATIO: What would you like to see?
If it's sorrow or woe, cease your search.

FIRST AMBASSADOR: The sight is dismal.

Our news from England comes too late.

The one who gave the order cannot hear.

Rosencrantz and Guildenstern are dead.

Now where will we get our thanks?

HORATIO *(pointing to the king)***:** Not from

His mouth, even if he could speak.

He never gave the order for their deaths.

I will tell you how all this happened.

FORTINBRAS: Let us hear it without delay.

I have some rights to this kingdom,

Which I shall now claim.

HORATIO: I shall also speak of that.

But for now, let us honor these dead.

FORTINBRAS: Let four captains

Carry Hamlet like a soldier. For his funeral,

Let soldiers' music and the rites of war

Speak loudly for him. Take up the bodies!

A sight like this belongs on a battlefield.

Here it seems out of place.

Go, bid the soldiers shoot.

(A salute of guns is fired. Drums beat. The bodies are
carried out. **All** exit.)

中文翻譯

簡介 P. 004

約五百年前，哈姆雷特的父親丹麥王被親生弟弟克勞地謀殺。接著，克勞地隨即娶了哈姆雷特的母親葛簇特。本劇開始時，哈姆雷特父親的鬼魂現身，告訴兒子兇手的身分，他要求哈姆雷特去報仇。隨著劇情發展，哈姆雷特試圖説服自己殺了克勞地。

本劇為莎士比亞最著名的劇本，以飽受精神折磨之苦的哈姆雷特一角聞名。

角色 P. 005

哈姆雷特，丹麥王儲：已故國王之子，也是現任丹麥國王之侄
克勞地，丹麥王儲：哈姆雷特的叔父
葛簇特：丹麥皇后，哈姆雷特之母
鬼魂：哈姆雷特被謀殺的父親之魂
波隆尼爾：克勞地的御前大臣
赫瑞修：平民，哈姆雷特的忠誠好友
雷爾提：波隆尼爾之子，歐菲莉亞之兄
歐菲莉亞：波隆尼爾之女，雷爾提之妹

羅生克蘭和蓋登思鄧：哈姆雷特的同學

傅特曼和康尼留斯：丹麥朝臣

馬賽勒、勃那多和弗蘭西斯科：城堡侍衛

雷納爾度：波隆尼爾的僕人

奧斯利克：丹麥朝臣

掘墓人、王公、侍從、演員和僕人

第一幕

● 第一場 ————————————————— P. 007

（弗蘭西斯科在艾辛諾爾堡前的崗位上，勃那多上。）

勃那多：十二點的鐘聲已響，換我來站哨吧，弗蘭西斯科。

弗蘭西斯科：感謝你來與我換班，天氣冷冽刺骨，令人鬱悶。

勃那多：今晚還算平靜吧？

弗蘭西斯科：連一隻老鼠都沒。

勃那多：那麼，晚安了，請要求站哨同伴加快動作。

弗蘭西斯科：我好似聽見他們的聲音了。

（赫瑞修和馬賽勒上，同時弗蘭西斯科下。）

馬賽勒：哈囉，勃那多！

勃那多：歡迎，赫瑞修和馬賽勒。

馬賽勒：那「東西」又出現了嗎？

勃那多：我什麼都沒看見。

馬賽勒：赫瑞修說這只是我們的想像，他不相信我們看過了兩次！所以藉著今晚與我們一同站哨，他得以親眼目睹。

赫瑞修：它不會出現的。

勃那多：坐一會吧，讓我們再跟你說一次我們連續兩晚看見的東西，昨晚，大約此時，半夜一點的鐘聲剛響……

馬賽勒：安靜！那東西又來了。

（鬼魂上，身著鎧甲。）

勃那多：祂看起來就像先王！

馬賽勒：跟祂說話吧，赫瑞修！

赫瑞修（對鬼魂說）：你是誰？你為什麼要身著這副鎧甲，我們的先王有時會穿它出巡。奉天之名，我命令你說話！

馬賽勒：祂好像被觸怒了。

勃那多：你看，祂要溜走了。

赫瑞修：請留步！開口吧！我命令你，開口說話吧！

（鬼魂下。）

馬賽勒：祂不會理你的，祂走了。

勃那多： 你現在感想如何，赫瑞修？你一直顫抖，臉色蒼白，這不都只是幻想罷了嗎？

赫瑞修： 老天在上，要不是我親眼看見，我絕對不會相信這事。

馬賽勒： 祂是不是很像先王？

赫瑞修： 如假包換！祂與雄心勃勃的挪威王作戰時，穿的正是那副鎧甲。他發怒時，也是如此皺眉的。真是太奇怪了，我不知要做何感想，但這似乎是不祥之兆。

馬賽勒： 說吧，若你了解原因所在，為何這位沉默且無法安息之魂這幾夜都來造訪，為何本國看似正處備戰狀態？

赫瑞修： 就我所知，我們的先王，也就是剛才出現的鬼魂，殺了挪威王老福丁布拉。他除了失去生命，也失去所有在戰爭中做為賭注的國土。若老福丁布拉戰勝，我們慈悲的先王則得放棄他的國土，這是他們的約定，所以很公平。現在老福丁布拉年輕的兒子小福丁布拉衝動、暴躁且愚蠢，組織一支毫無法紀的軍隊想收復父親失去的國土，這一定是我們備戰的原因，也是我們晚上得守夜的緣故。

勃那多： 我認為你是對的。

赫瑞修： 安靜！看啊！祂又來了！

（鬼魂再上。）

留下來吧，幻影！若你能出聲，與我對話吧。若你有任何事想請我幫忙，也告訴我吧。若你知曉你國家的命運，願意讓我們提前預知以避免災厄，喔，請你開口吧！

勃那多： 祂本來要開口了，但晨雞卻開始啼叫。

赫瑞修： 我聽說鬼魂得在白天時離開人間，而方才的景象證實此傳聞！太陽逐漸升起，我們的守衛工作已結束，讓我們向年輕的哈姆雷特報告今晚所見，我認為這位對我們沉默不語的鬼魂，將願意對他開口。

馬賓勒：就這麼做吧，我知道他人在何方。

（全員下。）

● **第二場** ————————————————— P. 012

（國王克勞地、皇后葛簇特、王子哈姆雷特、波隆尼爾、雷爾提、傅特曼、康尼留斯、眾臣和侍從們進入艾辛諾爾堡的議事大廳。）

國王：兄長去世的記憶仍舊猶新，我們的心充滿悽愴之情，但我們得為王國著想，本國因戰爭而風雨飄搖之際，需要領導者。因此，我將迎娶我的兄嫂為妻。現在，如各位所知，小福丁布拉認為我國正處於衰弱時期，他認為親愛兄長之死，令本國陷入混沌與混亂。他認為自己佔有優勢，不斷騷擾我們，要求我們歸還他父親輸給我兄長的國土，這也是召開本次會議的目的所在。我們已寫了要給挪威王的信，也就是小福丁布拉的叔父，他臥病在床，對其姪兒所為一無所知。我們要求他命令其姪兒別再騷擾我國，我們希望兩位，康尼留斯和傅特曼將，此信捎給挪威王。再會了，請盡速完成使命。

（國王克勞地將信交給他們。）

康尼留斯和傅特曼：遵命，陛下。

（他們鞠躬下。）

國王：雷爾提，你帶來什麼消息呢？你提到一項請求，是什麼呢？

雷爾提：仁慈的陛下，我想徵詢您的同意，讓我回到法國。我

132

自願來到此地參加您的登基大典，如今，我得坦白，既然使命已達，我再度希望能重返法國。

國王：雷爾提，你是否已徵得令尊的同意？波隆尼爾怎麼說呢？

波隆尼爾：陛下，他已徵得我的同意。

國王：好好享受年少時光吧，雷爾提，大好歲月就在你手中，恣意享用吧。現在，姪兒哈姆雷特，同時也是我兒⋯⋯

哈姆雷特（*旁白*）：我或許是你姪兒，但我永遠不會成為你兒。

國王：你為何如此抑鬱寡歡？

皇后：好哈姆雷特，拋開沉重的心情吧，萬物皆有一死，終究要落葉歸根回到永恆的。

哈姆雷特：是的，皇后陛下，我知道。

國王：你真是真情流露啊，哈姆雷特，如此悲戚地悼念令尊。但令尊也曾失去父親，他父親也是，你可以悲傷一段時日、但長久憑弔不但固執且沒有男子氣概，表示其心軟弱、焦躁，這可是犯天之錯，對亡者不敬，且違反自然定律。請拋開陰霾，視我們為父，讓所有人見證你是王位的繼承者，而我對你的疼愛，不會少於血脈相承的父子深情！你有意回到威登堡就學，卻與我們想法相左，我們想要求你留下，鼓舞我們並給予安慰，成為主要大臣、我姪兒，和我們的兒子。

皇后：求求你，哈姆雷特，留下來吧。

哈姆雷特：我會聽話的，母親。

國王：真是有心又聽話的回應啊。（**對皇后說：**）夫人，來吧。

（除了哈姆雷特，全體下。）

哈姆雷特：喔，但願我這身強壯的血肉之軀能化為露水，也但願自盡非罪。喔，神啊！喔，上帝啊！這世界實在令人生厭、乏味至極、了無新意且徒勞無功，就像疏於整理的花園，任憑雜草叢生。事情竟演變至此。父王去世才不到兩個月，是位明君，他深愛母后，甚至不願讓風吹襲她的臉龐。母親對他百般依賴，受他滋養有如生命靈糧。但一個月不到，算了，不想也罷。弱者，你的名字是女人！喔，老天，連沒有思考能力的禽獸都會哀悼更久！如今，你卻立刻嫁給叔父，我父親的弟弟，但兩人卻天差地遠，一如我與海立克士的差距。一個月未盡，她眼角的淚仍未風乾就已再嫁。喔，那速度之快！此婚姻必無法善終。心碎吧，我得沉默了。

（赫瑞修、馬賽勒和勃那多上。）

赫瑞修：王子殿下您好。

哈姆雷特：你好，赫瑞修，什麼風把你從威登堡吹來了？

赫瑞修：我來參加令尊的葬禮。

哈姆雷特：同窗，別諷刺我了，我以為你是來參加家母的婚禮。

赫瑞修：確實如此，婚禮緊接於葬禮之後。

哈姆雷特：為了節儉呀，赫瑞修。葬禮剩的菜餚還可繼續在婚禮使用，真希望那天永遠不會來臨，赫瑞修！我父親！我好像看到我父親了。

赫瑞修（驚訝貌）：殿下，在何處？

哈姆雷特：在我心中，赫瑞修。

赫瑞修：我與他有一面之緣，他是位明君。

哈姆雷特：從各方面來說，他都是位正人君子，但我再也看不到如此的君子風範了。

赫瑞修：殿下，我們昨晚似乎見到他了。

哈姆雷特：見到誰？

赫瑞修：殿下……是國王，令尊啊。

哈姆雷特：我父王？說來聽聽！

赫瑞修：好，聽著，讓我徐徐道來。馬賽勒和勃那多連續兩晚看見長相像令尊的形體，全身上下穿著盔甲。他們私下告訴我這個秘密，於是我於第三晚加入守夜，鬼魂又出現了。我認識令尊，鬼魂看起來確實像他。

哈姆雷特：你有跟他說話嗎？

赫瑞修：我有，但他沒有回應。

哈姆雷特：真是太奇怪了。

赫瑞修：殿下，我以個人名譽起誓，此事屬實，我們認為有責任告知您此事。

哈姆雷特：的確如此，但這讓我感到困惑，你們今天負責守夜嗎？

赫瑞修：是的，殿下。

哈姆雷特：你說他身著盔甲？

馬賽勒和勃那多：是啊，殿下。

哈姆雷特：但你們沒見到他的臉龐？

兩人：有，但他戴上半臉面甲。

哈姆雷特：他有蹙眉不悅嗎？

赫瑞修：他的表情較為哀戚而非憤怒。

哈姆雷特：真希望我也在場！今晚我要與你們一同守夜，也許鬼魂會再次現身，若他看似我尊貴的父親，我想與他談話。

請保守秘密，晚上見，我將於十一到十二點之間前往。

全體：到時見了，再見。

（赫瑞修、馬賽勒和勃那多下。）

哈姆雷特：父王的亡靈，還身穿盔甲！情況不太對勁，多希望夜幕已臨！在那之前，我要耐心以對。紙是包不住火的，惡行將被揭露。

（哈姆雷特下。）

● 第三場 ————————————————— P. 019

（雷爾提和歐菲莉亞進入波隆尼爾家中一室。）

雷爾提：行囊皆已上船，再會了。吾妹，請捎信來告知近況。

歐菲莉亞：你難道認為我不會嗎？

雷爾提：至於哈姆雷特與他對你的愛慕之意，切莫期望太高。好似春天的紫蘿蘭，快速綻放且甜美，但卻不持久，只有一時的馨香，如此而已。

歐菲莉亞：如此而已？

雷爾提：是的，也許他現在愛慕著你，但請小心，謹記他的地位。他不能順從自己的意志，不像他人，他也許無法隨心所欲。本國的安全與福祉緊繫於他所做的選擇，因此他必將以丹麥福祉為優先，而非婚姻。若他對你吐露愛意，請將這段話謹記於心，若你將心給了他或失去榮譽，你也會失去美名。請戒慎恐懼啊，歐菲莉亞，要審慎思量，我親愛的小妹，要小心情慾的危險。

歐菲莉亞：我會將你的話謹記於心，但吾兄，別帶我走上險峻且布滿荊棘的天堂之路，卻將自己口中的殷切勸言置於腦後。

（波隆尼爾上。）

波隆尼爾：雷爾提，你還在這兒呀？登船吧！上船去吧！若現在啟程你將一帆風順，你耽誤到眾人了。（手撫雷爾提的頭：）去吧！祝福你！給你一些建議，要對人友善，勿粗魯無禮。維繫友誼，用心深交，但別輕易向每位剛認識的人伸出友誼之手。傾聽眾人之見，多聽少言，聆聽批評，卻不評斷他人。買衣裝時量入為出，以品質為重，避免花俏俗氣——衣裝可以傳達許多個人訊息。不要與他人有借貸關係，借出錢財常令人同時失去錢財與友誼，而向人借錢則容易使自己揮霍成性。但最重要的是：要忠於自我，一如黑夜追隨白晝，也不要虧待他人。再會了，我的祝福與你同在。

雷爾提：那麼我就恭敬不如從命了，父親。（對歐菲莉亞：）再會了，歐菲莉亞，記得我的叮嚀。

歐菲莉亞：我已將你的話深鎖於心，而你握有開啟鎖匙。

（雷爾提下。）

波隆尼爾：歐菲莉亞，他對你說了什麼呢？

歐菲莉亞：關於哈姆雷特王子之事。

波隆尼爾：我想也是，我聽說你與哈姆雷特最近交往甚密，若此事屬實，我得說你不了解可能產生的流言蜚語。你們之間究竟是什麼情況呢？告訴我實情吧。

歐菲莉亞：父親，他已向我表示愛慕之情。

波隆尼爾：愛慕之情？哈！你還蠢到相信他？

歐菲莉亞：他以君子風範展開追求，且言行一致，如神聖起誓般守信。

波隆尼爾：這些誓言如鳥籠般脆弱，別輕易相信他。從現在開始，你切莫如此輕浮隨便，也別再與他單獨相會，我甚至不希望你與他交談，這是命令，改變行事吧。

歐菲莉亞：我會照做的，父親。

（波隆尼爾和歐菲莉亞下。）

●第四場 ────────────────── P. 023

（哈姆雷特、赫瑞修和馬賽勒進入城堡前的空地。）

哈姆雷特：寒風刺骨，十分寒冷。現在幾點了？

赫瑞修：好像快午夜了。

馬賽勒：不，已過午夜了。

赫瑞修：是嗎？那麼現在已屆鬼魂現身遊蕩之時。

（鬼魂上。）

赫瑞修：看啊，王子殿下，它來了！

哈姆雷特：願天使保佑吾等，無論你來意是善是惡，我想與你交談，我會稱呼你為哈姆雷特、國王、父王、高貴的丹麥人。喔，回答我吧！為何您的高貴身軀不好好安息，為何您的大理石墓打開讓您重返人間呢？你全副武裝遊蕩人世的原因究竟為何？說吧，為什麼呢？我們該如何是好？

（鬼魂向哈姆雷特示意。）

赫瑞修：它示意您過去。

馬賽勒：別跟鬼魂走。

赫瑞修：千萬別去。

哈姆雷特：我若不隨它去，它就不開口。

赫瑞修：王子殿下，別照做。

哈姆雷特：為什麼，我何須懼怕？我的生命一文不值，至於我的靈魂，它也莫可奈何，它又向我招手了，我將跟隨它。

赫瑞修：若它領你走向危險之境或讓你陷入瘋狂該怎辦？請小心！

哈姆雷特：它仍然在對我招手。（對鬼魂說：）走吧，我跟你走。

馬賽勒（拉住他）：殿下，別去。

哈姆雷特：把手放下。

赫瑞修：請聽我們的話，千萬別去。

哈姆雷特：命運已召喚我，讓我血脈賁張，如雄獅之勇。（鬼魂示意。）放手吧，同伴。（掙脫。）誰敢擋我的路，我就讓他下九泉！我命令你，讓開！（對鬼魂說：）走吧，我跟你走。

（鬼魂和哈姆雷特下。）

馬賽勒：我們跟著他走。

赫瑞修：這樣有什麼好處？

馬賽勒：正有齷齪之事在丹麥發生。

赫瑞修：上天自會處理！

馬賽勒：不，我們尾隨他去吧。

（赫瑞修和馬賽勒下。）

●第五場 ──────────────────── P. 026

（鬼魂和哈姆雷特前往城堡偏僻之處。）

哈姆雷特：你要領我去何方呢？開口吧！我不願再往前行。

鬼魂：仔細聽我說。

哈姆雷特：我會的。

鬼魂：時辰將至，我將回到痛苦的烈火中。

哈姆雷特：太悲慘了，可憐的幽靈。

鬼魂：別可憐我，請仔細聽我將吐露之事。

哈姆雷特：說吧！我將側耳傾聽。

鬼魂：你聽罷後，請展開復仇。

哈姆雷特：什麼意思？

鬼魂：我是你父王的亡靈，註定夜間在外遊蕩，白日則被困在烈火中，直到煉淨我這生的罪孽後才得以解脫。若我不被允許從這禁錮牢籠中透露秘密，那麼我就來訴說一個讓你直冒冷汗、目瞪口呆、怒髮衝冠且毛骨悚然的故事，但你不可洩露此事給其他血肉之軀。若你敬愛你的父王，請聽我道來……

哈姆雷特：喔，天啊。

鬼魂：為他卑劣且有違人倫的謀殺復仇。

哈姆雷特：謀殺！

鬼魂：謀殺是最惡劣的罪行，一向如此。但這一件是最邪惡、詭譎且違反人倫的謀殺案。

哈姆雷特：請告訴我事情經過，讓我帶著您的愛，踏著飛步為您報仇。

鬼魂：哈姆雷特，請聽我説。傳言一條蟒蛇趁著我在果園沉睡時咬我一口，這傳遍全丹麥的説法是天大謊言。請了解，你這高貴的年輕人，真正取走你父親性命之人，即是頭戴冠冕的那位。

哈姆雷特：喔，跟我想的一樣！是我叔父！

鬼魂：沒錯，就是那禽獸。他先縱容無恥的慾望，贏得我皇后的芳心，喔，哈姆雷特，她竟如此沉淪！我對她的愛如此聖潔真摯，她卻自甘墮落愛上那位遠不如我的惡人。時間不多了，我已聞到晨間氣息，我將長話短説。我正在果園小睡，這是我午後的習慣，而你叔父潛身靠近我，在我耳內倒入劇毒，那毒快而致命，如水銀般迅速流竄全身，令我立刻斷氣。因此，我在熟睡時被胞弟親手所弒，轉瞬奪走我的性命、王位和皇后，連臨終懺悔都來不及，就取走我的命，讓我滿身罪孽地會見造物主，實在太恐怖、太慘，且太駭人。

若你感到忿忿不平，切莫忍耐，別讓丹麥的皇室眠床成為奢侈與亂倫的臥榻。但不管你將如何行動，別傷害你的母親，把她交給上天，讓她因良心不安而受苦。我得立刻離開了，黎明將至，再會，再會！哈姆雷特，別忘了我！

（鬼魂下。）

哈姆雷特：別忘了你！當然不會，可憐的魂魄！我將從記憶中抹除所有愚蠢的回憶、書中建言，和所有從年少青春和觀察汲取的寶貴知識。只有您的訓誡將永駐腦海，不被瑣事所擾。喔，可惡至極的女人！喔，惡人，惡人，滿臉奸笑的惡人！邪惡至極的奸人。至少我相信，或許在丹麥就有這種人，而叔父那就是你，我會切守誓言，勿忘父王，我以此為誓。

赫瑞修（從後台）：殿下，王子殿下！

馬賽勒（從後台）：哈姆雷特王子！

赫瑞修（從後台）：上天救救他呀！

（赫瑞修和馬賽勒上。）

馬賽勒：怎麼了，王子殿下？

赫瑞修：有什麼消息嗎，殿下？

哈姆雷特：喔，極好的消息！

赫瑞修：殿下，告訴我們吧。

哈姆雷特：不，你們會說溜嘴。

赫瑞修：我不會，我對上天起誓。

馬賽勒：我也不會，殿下。

哈姆雷特：你們將保守秘密嗎？

赫瑞修和馬賽勒：是的，殿下。

哈姆雷特：丹麥有位惡人。

赫瑞修：殿下，此事不用鬼魂出墳告訴我們。

哈姆雷特：喔，你說的對，讓我們互相握手道別吧。你們去處理份內的事，我也去忙我的。好友們，既然你們身為我的摯友、學者和士兵，請應允我一項請求。

赫瑞修：是什麼呢，殿下？我們將答應您。

哈姆雷特：千萬別洩漏今晚所見之事。

赫瑞修和馬賽勒：我們不會的。

哈姆雷特：按著我的寶劍起誓吧

馬賽勒：我們已立過誓言，殿下。

哈姆雷特：是的，但按我的寶劍起誓吧，快起誓。

鬼魂（從台下）：起誓吧。

哈姆雷特：快！聽見那地底傳來的幽魂聲嗎？起誓吧。

赫瑞修：殿下，請表明誓言。

哈姆雷特：永不洩漏今晚所見之事，按著我的寶劍起誓。

鬼魂（從台下）：起誓吧。

哈姆雷特：兩位請上前來，將你們的手按在我寶劍上，發誓永不洩漏今晚所見之事，按劍起誓吧。

鬼魂（從台下）：起誓吧。

哈姆雷特：說得好，老傢伙。好友們，再立一次誓。

赫瑞修：喔，這真是太詭異了！

哈姆雷特：即使詭異，也得接受，世上有許多怪事，赫瑞修，比你所夢之哲理還多。但如過往般上前吧，起誓吧。

鬼魂（從台下）：起誓吧。

哈姆雷特：安息吧，安息吧，被俗事所擾的冤魂。（赫瑞修和馬賽勒起誓。）好的，兩位，我對你們滿心關懷且感謝，讓我們一同進去城堡吧。切記，一字都不可洩漏，世事紛亂，喔，多可惡啊！我降世即背負撥亂為正的命運！現在走吧，讓我們一同離開。

（全體下。）

第二幕

●第一場 ──────────────── P. 035

（波隆尼爾和雷納爾度進入波隆尼爾家中一室。）

波隆尼爾：在你拜訪雷爾提前，先打聽人們對他的看法。也許可以如此詢問：『我與雷爾提不熟，對他只略知一二，他看似是位狂野之徒，沉迷於諸如此類。』你可以任意捏造不良嗜好，但切莫毀損他的名聲。

雷納爾度：像賭博可以嗎？

波隆尼爾：可以，或嗜酒和爭鬥，一些年輕人常有的荒唐行徑。用輕描淡寫的方式講述他的缺點，形容那只是一時血氣方剛。當你訴說小犬的輕微過犯時，跟你交談的人也許會回應：『我認識這位年輕人，我昨日或某天前有見到他，他跟某人在一起，而如你所説，他正在賭博。』你聽，現在你撒下的謊言誘餌，已釣到真相之魚。我只想知道他平日的所做所為，你聽懂了嗎？

雷納爾度：我聽懂了。

波隆尼爾：再會了，幫我盯著他。

（雷納爾度下，歐菲莉亞上。）

波隆尼爾：歐菲莉亞，怎麼了？

歐菲莉亞：喔，父親，我感到十分害怕！

波隆尼爾：老天，是什麼事呢？

歐菲莉亞：我方才在房間縫紉，哈姆雷特王子入內，上衣開襟未釦，頂上無帽，襪子骯髒無比，且落於腳踝，表情驚慌，看似發狂。

波隆尼爾：因愛你而發狂嗎？

歐菲莉亞：父親，我不曉得，但看似如此。

波隆尼爾：他説了什麼？

歐菲莉亞：他緊握住我的手腕，直瞪著我的臉看，彷彿要為我作畫。過了好一陣子他都是這樣，最後他搖動我的手臂，發出一聲嘆息，並讓我離開。接著他轉頭離去，離開時他不斷回頭望我，根本沒在看路，最後，他又盯著我看。

波隆尼爾：跟我走，把此事稟報國王吧，如此的愛十分危險，會讓人做出絕望的瘋狂之舉，你最近有對他口出任何嚴厲之言嗎？

歐菲莉亞：父親，我沒有，但如你要求，我拒絕他的情書，且不再與他相處。

波隆尼爾：這就是使他發狂的原因，很抱歉，我看錯他了。我以為他只是玩弄你的感情，並存心害你，也許是我忌妒心使然。我們去見國王吧，我們得稟告他。若此事被隱瞞，可能會導致你我不願見到的悲慘後果。

（歐菲莉亞和波隆尼爾下。）

●第二場 ——————————— P. 038

（國王、皇后、羅生克蘭、蓋登思鄧和侍從們進入城堡一室。）

國王：歡迎，親愛的羅生克蘭和蓋登思鄧！我們十分思念兩位！我們要求兩位盡速前來，是由於我們需要兩位相助。你們已聽聞哈姆雷特的改變，他從裡到外判若兩人，其緣由除了父親去世之外，我百思不解。你倆跟他年紀相仿，且從小與他一同長大，我想請兩位來皇宮小住一番，花點時間陪伴他，也許你們會了解問題所在。我們了解後，也許可以設法幫他。

皇后：兩位，他在言談中有提到你們，我想再也沒有其他人能討他開心，若兩位願意在此小住，你們將收到豐厚的獎賞。

羅生克蘭：不需獎賞。

蓋登思鄧：我們很樂意相助。

國王：感謝，羅生克蘭和蓋登思鄧。

皇后：感謝，蓋登思鄧和羅生克蘭。懇求你們立刻造訪我那位性情大變的兒子。

（羅生克蘭和蓋登思鄧下，波隆尼爾上。）

波隆尼爾：親愛的陛下，出使挪威來大使已歡天喜地地回國。

國王：你總是捎來好消息！

波隆尼爾：是嗎，陛下？陛下，我向您擔保我的職責一如我的
靈魂般神聖，我想我已找出哈姆雷特發狂的主因。

國王：喔，說到這件事，我很想聽聽。

波隆尼爾：您先跟大使談談吧，我的消息用來錦上添花即可。

國王：很好，宣他們晉見。（波隆尼爾下。）（對皇后說：）他跟我
說他知道哈姆雷特行為怪異的原因。

皇后：我以為原因再明顯不過——是他父親的死和我們迅速
的再婚。

國王：讓我們聽聽波隆尼爾的說法。（波隆尼爾與傅特曼和康尼
留斯上。）歡迎各位好友！說吧，傅特曼，你從挪威捎來什麼
消息呢？

傅特曼：挪威王以為他侄兒正準備出兵波蘭，但當他開始留
意，他發現侄兒的確想揮兵進攻陛下，他要求小福丁布拉
住手。簡而言之，小福丁布拉遵從並誓言永不對您作戰。於
是，開心的挪威王決定挹注一筆資金讓小福丁布拉帶兵討
伐波蘭。（傅特曼遞給國王一份文件。）挪威王想要求您准許他
侄兒於征討波蘭時，帶兵穿越我國領土。

國王：等我們有閒工夫再來詳讀、回應並考慮此事吧。在那之
前，我們感謝你的付出，去歇息吧，今晚我們將一同歡宴。

（傅特曼和康尼留斯下。）

波隆尼爾：那真是好消息！現在，既然言貴簡潔，我將長話短
　　說。您尊貴的王子已發瘋。這是事實，令人難過；雖令人惋
　　惜，卻是事實。但重點是，讓我們承認他已瘋的事實，我們
　　必須找出此事之肇因，或是此病之肇因。我女兒將此信交
　　給我。（波隆尼爾出示一封信。）現在，請聆聽並思考。（朗誦。）
　　『致美若天仙且讓我全心崇拜的歐菲莉亞。』（評論該信。）
　　那真是愚蠢且邪惡的字眼，『美麗』是個粗鄙的詞彙，但
　　是且聽我說。（再次朗誦。）『你可懷疑繁星如火，懷疑烈日
　　不移，懷疑真理之假，但千萬別懷疑我的愛。喔歐菲莉亞，
　　我不擅言詞，但請相信我對你至深的愛，無與倫比，請相
　　信我。再會了。我將永屬於你，親愛的淑女。哈姆雷特筆。』

（他將信紙摺起來。）

　　我女兒因順服我的要求，把這封信給我看。

國王：你女兒是如何接受他的愛意？

波隆尼爾：當我一得知此事，我立刻告訴小女：『哈姆雷特殿
　　下是王子，你配不上他，此事萬萬不可。』然後我告誡她，
　　要她拒哈姆雷特於門外，不得接見任何信差，婉拒禮物。
　　她聽從我的建議，而他則陷入悲傷，接著絕食，身心疲弱，

行為輕浮，由此，他陷入讓我們眾人悲嘆的瘋癲狀態。

國王：你認為這就是原因所在？

皇后：或許如此，可能性極高。

波隆尼爾：難道我以前曾說錯過？

國王：印象中沒有，我們要如何試驗你的說法？

波隆尼爾：他有時會在大廳內獨步數小時。

皇后：他的確會這麼做。

波隆尼爾：當他這麼做時，我將確保小女就在附近。你我將躲
在簾幕後方觀看他倆的會面，若他不愛她，並且不因此失
去理智，那我將辭官歸隱下田耕作。

國王：就如此行吧。

（哈姆雷特上，正在讀書。）

皇后：看他的面容如此憔悴地看書。

波隆尼爾：離開吧，我懇求你們，你們兩位都是。我現在就去
找他商談，請迴避。（國王、皇后及侍從下。）哈姆雷特殿下，您
好嗎？

哈姆雷特：很好，感謝上蒼。

波隆尼爾：您認識我嗎，殿下？

哈姆雷特：是的，你是位狡猾的漁販。

波隆尼爾：殿下，我不是那樣的人。

哈姆雷特：那麼我希望你為人是那樣真誠。

波隆尼爾：真誠，殿下？

哈姆雷特：是的，閣下，在這世上，誠實之人萬中無一。

波隆尼爾：此話確實無誤，殿下。

哈姆雷特：你有女兒嗎？

波隆尼爾：殿下，我有。

哈姆雷特：別讓她走在烈陽之下，拋頭露面會導致傷害。

波隆尼爾：您指的是什麼呢？（竊語）言談之際仍是吾女，但他
　　起初沒認出我，他以為我是魚販。他已病入膏肓，的確，我
　　輕狂年少時，也曾如此因愛而苦，我再與他談談。（對哈姆雷
　　特說：）殿下，您在讀什麼呢？

哈姆雷特：文字、文字、全是文字。

波隆尼爾：殿下，是關於什麼呢？

哈姆雷特：關於誰之間的事嗎？

波隆尼爾：我是說，您看的書是關於什麼？

哈姆雷特：謊言啊，閣下。作者說老人有灰白的鬍子，佈滿皺
　　紋的臉龐和經常流淚的雙目。但他也說老人缺乏智慧，雙
　　腿無力。這一切我皆全心相信，但我認為這不該被寫下。

波隆尼爾（竊語）：雖然他滿口胡言，卻仍富有邏輯。（對哈姆雷
　　特說：）殿下，恕我得請你讓我離去。

哈姆雷特：閣下，你要請我給你什麼我都欣然願意，除了我的
　　性命，除了性命，除了我的小命……

波隆尼爾：再會了，殿下。

（波隆尼爾下。）

哈姆雷特：這些令人厭煩的老糊塗。

（羅生克蘭和蓋登思鄧上。）

哈姆雷特：好友們，有何新消息嗎？

羅生克蘭：沒有，殿下，但全世界卻變得耿直誠實。

哈姆雷特：那麼世界末日已近！但你的消息並不正確。讓我問你一個問題，你究竟惹上何事，讓幸運女神送你來此牢籠？

蓋登思鄧：殿下，牢籠？

哈姆雷特：丹麥是個牢籠。

羅生克蘭：那麼這個世界也是。

哈姆雷特：世界是個大牢籠，有許多囚室與地牢，但丹麥是其中最糟糕的。

羅生克蘭：我們並不如此認為，殿下。

哈姆雷特：那麼，這對兩位而言也許並非牢籠，因為世上本無好壞之分，除非人們認為如此，對我而言，這裡是個牢籠。

羅生克蘭：那麼您的抱負讓此地成為牢籠，丹麥對您而言不過是豆大之地。

哈姆雷特：喔，老天，我願意住在核果殼中，並自立為擁有無限領土的君王，但我的夢境通常充滿災厄。

蓋登思鄧：那些夢境的確與雄心有關，因為雄心壯志只是夢境幻影。

哈姆雷特：夢境本身即是幻境。

羅生克蘭：的確如此，我也相信雄心空虛飄渺，不過是幻影之影。

哈姆雷特：我們去宮廷中吧？因我實在不願再思索這事了。

羅生克蘭和蓋登思鄧：我們將侍奉您。

哈姆雷特：不，不需要。我不會將你們與我僕人視為同類，老實說，我是位難伺候的人。但我們友誼甚篤，你們為何前來艾辛諾爾呢？

羅生克蘭：來看您呀，沒有其他原因了。

哈姆雷特：謝謝，但說真的，親愛的朋友們，你們真的不是被請來的嗎？說吧，吐露真相，說吧，說吧，告訴我吧！

蓋登思鄧：殿下，您要我們說什麼呢？

哈姆雷特：說什麼都行，但請回答問題。你們是被派來的對吧，我知道國王與皇后請你們前來。

羅生克蘭：殿下，緣故何在？

哈姆雷特：你說呢？看在同窗情誼，對我說真話吧。你們是否是被請來的？

蓋登思鄧：殿下，我們是被請來的。

哈姆雷特：讓我來說原因吧，如此你們就不需背著國王皇后洩露秘密。近來，為著我不明白的緣故，我失去一切樂趣並停止強健身心。的確，我甚感痛苦，世上對我而言乏味無趣。而這股清風，在我看來不過是一團廢氣。人類是上天如此偉大的藝品！因著高尚的緣故被創！智慧超群！無論形體或儀態皆令人讚嘆！行動有如天使！仔細思索，多麼像神！舉世非凡！萬物之靈！但由我看來，這不過是一身塵土嗎？人不能再帶給我歡樂，非也，女人亦若如此，雖然由你的笑容看來，你不同意。

羅生克蘭：我絕無如此想法。

哈姆雷特：那麼你為何在我說『人不能再帶給我歡樂』時笑？

羅生克蘭：殿下，我只是在思索，若無人能帶給你歡樂，那麼您將對稍後將至的演員們不屑一顧了。

哈姆雷特：什麼樣的演員？

羅生克蘭：您十分喜愛的那類——從大城來的悲劇演員。

哈姆雷特：他們為何要巡迴演出？他們在城市時佳評如潮，名利雙收？他們仍如我在城市時那般受歡迎嗎？

羅生克蘭：不，沒有。

哈姆雷特：為何？難道他們演技生疏了嗎？

羅生克蘭：不，他們演技仍老練，但出現了一組新的兒童演員，目前大受好評，引領風騷。

哈姆雷特：兒童演員？誰照顧他們？誰餵飽他們？當他們長大變聲時會退出劇團嗎？等他們日後成為一般的演員後，會責怪劇作家嗎？

羅生克蘭：眾說紛紜，但無人知道問題解決之道，但這正是悲劇演員巡演之因。

（台下喇叭聲宣布演員的到來。）

蓋登思鄧：演員到了。

哈姆雷特：各位先生，歡迎來到艾辛諾爾，但我的叔叔及父和嬸嬸及母親被我欺騙。

蓋登思鄧：怎麼說呢，殿下？

哈姆雷特：我只在吹北北西風時瘋癲，當南風吹彿時，我便能辨清是非。

（波隆尼爾上。）

波隆尼爾：各位好。

哈姆雷特（對羅生克蘭和蓋登思鄧悄聲說）：那個老嬰孩仍未脫襁褓呢。

羅生克蘭（對哈姆雷特悄聲說）：也許那位老先生正返老還童。

哈姆雷特（竊語）：我猜他是來告訴我演員之事，且聽他說。（對波隆尼爾說：）閣下你好。

波隆尼爾：殿下，演員來了。

哈姆雷特：是這樣嗎？

波隆尼爾：我用名譽起誓。

（四或五位演員上。）

哈姆雷特：歡迎，先生們！歡迎各位！（對波隆尼爾說：）閣下，可否請你確保他們有好的居所？讓他們梳洗休息一番。

波隆尼爾：殿下，我會的，各位請跟我來。

哈姆雷特：請隨他走，朋友們，我們明日再看戲。

（波隆尼爾與演員下，只留第一演員，哈姆雷特對留下來的演員說話。）

哈姆雷特：你能演《貢札古之死》嗎？

第一演員：可以，殿下。

哈姆雷特：明晚請你們演出此劇。我想寫十二到十六行台詞加入劇本中，你可以加以詳讀研究，可否辦到？

第一演員：可以的，殿下。

哈姆雷特：很好。（指向波隆尼爾離開之處：）隨那位先生去吧，別嘲弄他。（第一演員下，哈姆雷特與羅生克蘭和蓋登思鄧對話。）今晚見，歡迎蒞臨艾辛諾爾。

羅生克蘭：謝謝，殿下。

（羅生克蘭和蓋登思鄧下。）

哈姆雷特：獨剩敝人。喔，我真是位惡棍！我難道是怯懦之人嗎？一定是的，否則我早已將國王屍首餵食鳥禽——那卑鄙至極的惡人！喔，復仇！我親愛父王被害身亡，身為其子，天地鬼神催我復仇，我卻只能用文字抒發心事。聽說心虛之畜看戲時，會因劇情與所作所為相仿而良心發現，有時會自首其邪惡之行。我將要求這些演員在叔父面前，上演類似我父被弒的情節。我會察言觀色，若他有所反應，我將知道該如何做。或許我所見之靈實為惡魔，因惡魔時常以討喜外表出沒，也許因我軟弱與悲傷之故，它想領我走上邪惡之路。我雖想信任那魂魄，但我卻無法確認那魂魄為我父之靈，我需要更多確據，藉由此劇我將測試國王良知。

（哈姆雷特下。）

第三幕

●第一場 ──────────────────── P. 055

（國王、皇后、波隆尼爾、歐菲莉亞、羅生克蘭和蓋登思鄧進入城堡一室。）

國王：哈姆雷特是否有向你吐露行事古怪之因？

羅生克蘭：他說他精神恍惚，卻不肯透露原因。

皇后：他有對任何消遣娛樂產生興趣嗎？

羅生克蘭：夫人，我們來此途中恰好遇上一些演員，我們告知哈姆雷特此事，他聽聞此消息時流露出一絲喜悅之情。演員們目前都在宮中，據我所知已被吩咐於今晚為他演戲。

波隆尼爾：沒錯，他請我邀請陛下於今晚一同看戲。

國王：我滿心樂意，很高興得知他對事物產生興趣。先生們，告訴他我們將蒞臨參加。

羅生克蘭：遵命，陛下。

（羅生克蘭和蓋登思鄧下。）

國王：親愛的葛簇特，你也先迴避一下吧。我們已請哈姆雷特

前來，與歐菲莉亞來場不期而遇。她的父親與我將擔任密
探，在暗地觀察他倆，希望藉由他的言行來評判他是否被
愛所困。

皇后：我將照做。（對歐菲莉亞說：）歐菲莉亞，我誠心希望你的
美貌是讓哈姆雷特瘋癲的緣故，我也希望你的美德能讓他
恢復理智——為了你倆的名譽。

歐菲莉亞：夫人，我也希望如此。

（皇后下。）

波隆尼爾：歐菲莉亞，到這邊來。閱讀這本祈禱書吧，莫讓人
因你落單而感到奇怪。（對國王說：）我聽見他來了。

（國王和波隆尼爾下，哈姆雷特上。）

哈姆雷特：生存抑或是死亡，大哉問也。讓內心承受命運無情
的打擊較為高尚？或是該起身反抗無盡煩擾，奮鬥並終結
苦難？死亡即是長眠，別無其他，而這場酣眠能了結心碎與
肉體的震撼衝擊，是令人滿心期盼的結局。死亡即是長眠，

沉睡⋯⋯或是做場大夢。唉，但這就是窒礙所在，在死亡長眠中，所夢為何？這些想法令人裏足不前。為何要忍受時間的磨難？為何要受苦於愛戀的折磨並且受狂人之辱？這一切用匕首即可了斷。其緣故在於人們懼怕死後世界，那從未有人返回的未知國度。恐懼糊塗了意志，令人甘願忍受痛苦，而非進入未知境界，良知使人懦弱。（他見到歐菲莉亞。）美麗的歐菲莉亞！請在禱告中為我懺悔。

歐菲莉亞：殿下，我想退還您的贈禮，請收下吧。

哈姆雷特：不，非我，我從未送你任何禮物。

歐菲莉亞：您明知您曾如此，您還用甜言蜜語增添禮物的豐盛，如今芬香已失，請將禮物收回吧。因為對於自重之人，薄情贈禮者使厚禮消薄。

哈姆雷特：我曾深愛過你。

歐菲莉亞：您也讓我深信於此。

哈姆雷特：你不該相信我的巧語，我不再愛你了！

歐菲莉亞：那麼我確確實實地被欺騙了。

哈姆雷特：出家吧！何苦成為罪人之母呢？為何如我這般之人得沉浮於天地之間？我們皆非善類，全是如此，千萬別相信吾等。出家去吧！但若你得嫁人，讓我給你此建言：若你守貞如玉，純潔如雪，終究仍逃不過流言蜚語，快出家去吧！

歐菲莉亞：上天賜我力量，讓他恢復正常。

哈姆雷特：或者，若你非得嫁人，嫁個傻子吧，聰明人能看穿你的邪惡。這樣好了，大家都別結婚了。那些已婚之人，可以繼續美滿婚姻的只有一人，其他人則維持現狀。出家吧——快去！

（哈姆雷特下。）

歐菲莉亞：如此高尚之人已失去理智！我是天下最可憐的女子，曾聽聞他悅耳的愛語，如今樂音卻荒腔走調，喔，不幸如我，親眼目睹我所見到的一切。

（國王與波隆尼爾上。）

國王：他的想法並非出自於愛戀！他談話的神情——也不像瘋言瘋語。在他靈魂深處藏有悲傷，如母雞孵卵，當卵孵化，危險將至。若欲避免，我有一計畫。哈姆雷特將啟程去英格蘭，英格蘭國王積欠我國債務，哈姆雷特將去追討。也許漂洋過海和不同國度將讓哈姆雷特恢復正常。波隆尼爾，你對此計意下如何？

波隆尼爾：此計應當能行，但我仍深信他的悲傷來自失戀。陛下，請隨心所欲，但容我建議：在表演過後，讓皇后私下與他會面，也許她能讓王子暢所欲言。我將躲在一旁竊聽，若她仍無法探知他悲傷之因，再派他至英格蘭——或將他監禁於您認為的合適之處。

國王：就這麼辦吧，如此嚴重的瘋癲不得不加以注意。

（全體下。）

●第二場 P. 061

（哈姆雷特與某些演員進入城堡一室。）

哈姆雷特：照著我朗讀的方式說出對白，字正腔圓、不疾不徐，若你如其它演員般吼叫，我還不如請城鎮傳令官幫我念台詞。別揮舞四肢，手勢要輕柔，自然流暢的演出較好，但也別演得索然無味。請自行判斷，令手勢搭配台詞，台詞合乎手勢。謹記表演是真實人生的映照，換句話說，請忠實呈現，去做準備吧。

（演員下，赫瑞修上。）

哈姆雷特：你好嗎，赫瑞修？

赫瑞修：殿下，還不錯，我在此靜候吩咐。

哈姆雷特：赫瑞修，你是我見過最明理的人了。

赫瑞修：喔，親愛的殿下……

哈姆雷特：我說這話不是要恭維你，這樣做對我有何益處呢？你雖身無長物，卻受樂觀積極的態度滋養。怎會有人要恭維窮人呢？從我學會識人後，我擇你為友。即便你遭逢了不幸，卻從不抱怨，總對好事壞事一同獻上感激之意。無視命運捉弄，而仍勇往直前的人實有福氣。倘若有他人也是如此不受情緒左右，我將全心珍重此人，如我看重你般！今晚在國王面前將有齣戲要上演，其中一幕與我父之死非常相像，如我之前向你吐露那般。當你見到該劇情上演，請觀察我叔父，若他在那時仍將平日隱藏的愧疚感不形於色，我將會感到吃驚。我也將仔細端詳他的面容，待戲終，我倆再一起比較所見之事。

赫瑞修：好的，殿下。

哈姆雷特：我聽見他們前來演戲的聲響了，我得開始裝瘋賣傻，去入席而坐吧。

（台下傳來號角聲，宣告國王和皇后駕到。國王、皇后、波隆尼爾、羅生克蘭、蓋登思鄧和其餘人等上。）

國王：哈姆雷特，今晚好嗎？

哈姆雷特：很好，真的。就像變色龍，以空氣為食，對未來充滿希望。雞可就不能這麼養了。

國王：你講的話毫無章理，哈姆雷特。

哈姆雷特：對我亦是如此，演員們都準備好了嗎？

羅生克蘭：是的，殿下。

皇后：來吧，親愛的哈姆雷特，坐我身旁。

哈姆雷特：不，親愛的母后，有其他事更吸引我。

波隆尼爾（對國王說）：你聽見了嗎？

哈姆雷特（對歐菲莉亞說）：女士，我可否躺臥在你大腿中。

（他躺臥在歐菲莉亞的腳邊。）

歐菲莉亞（害羞貌）：不行啊，殿下。

哈姆雷特：我是說，將頭枕在你的大腿上。

歐菲莉亞：可以的，殿下。您心情真不錯，殿下。

哈姆雷特：心情為何不好呢？看我母親飛揚的神色，而我父親
　　不過才剛去世兩小時。

歐菲莉亞：才不，已經四個月了，殿下。

哈姆雷特：如此之久？喔老天啊！才去世兩個月卻仍未被遺
　　忘？那麼如此偉人的事蹟也許會被傳誦，時間將比他有生
　　之年更長。

（台下傳來喇叭聲，啞劇演員上。戲中國王和戲中皇后深情擁抱，他將
頭靠在她肩上，她將他臥在布滿花朵的床上，她見他熟睡便離去。不
久後，來了一名男子，將戲中國王皇冠摘下，親吻它，並將毒液倒進戲
中國王耳中，離去。戲中皇后返回，發現戲中國王已死，放聲哭嚎。下
毒者再次返回，與其他三四人一起，好似與她一同哀悼。屍首被移走，
兇手以禮追求戲中皇后，好一陣子，她看似不情不願，但最終接受他
的追求。所有演員下。）

歐菲莉亞：這是什麼意思，殿下？

哈姆雷特：這是惡作劇。

（讀序詩者上。）

讀序詩者：僅代表吾等與本劇，願各位喜歡今日所見，現在本
　　劇將演，莫再推延。

歐菲莉亞：這段話真簡潔，殿下。

哈姆雷特：如女人的愛戀般短暫。

（戲中國王和戲中皇后上。）

戲中國王：自我們攜手成婚轉眼已三十載。

戲中皇后：願此良緣結束前仍有三十載！但悲慘如我，您健康
　　大不如前，一如我對您愛意之深，我的恐懼也深。

戲中國王：是啊，我很快得離你而去，吾愛。你將繼續在我身
　　後於這繁華世界生活，我敬重又親愛的妻子，願你下位夫
　　婿也如我般疼愛你……

戲中皇后：喔，別再這麼說！若我再婚，我願受咒詛！因為只有
　　弒夫之婦才會再婚。

哈姆雷特（竊語）：真令人痛苦！

戲中皇后：再婚之因只為財利，而非愛情。當第二任丈夫親吻
　　我時，就猶如再度手刃第一任丈夫。

戲中國王：我知道你現在心口如一，但日後就算海誓山盟也會
　　破碎。世事難以長久，因此倘若改日你我之情不再，也不需
　　詫異。你認為你將無夫可改嫁，但待第一任丈夫死後，也許
　　你將改變心意。

戲中皇后：親愛的，我發誓此話為真：你是我終身唯一所愛。

戲中國王：多麼沉重的誓約！親愛的，離我而去吧！我得睡了。

（他沉睡。）

戲中皇后：親愛的，願安眠，願你我永不分離。

（戲中皇后下。）

哈姆雷特（對皇后說）：你還喜歡嗎？

皇后：我覺得女子所言過重。

哈姆雷特：喔，但她會信守諾言的。

國王：你曾看過這齣劇嗎？有什麼讓人不舒服的劇情嗎？

哈姆雷特：不，沒有！他們只是在演戲罷了，毒藥是假的，並無
　　冒犯之意。

國王：此劇劇名叫什麼呢？

哈姆雷特：《捕鼠器》，改編自維也納的謀殺案，貢札古是公
　　爵之名，其妻名為巴蒂絲塔。請繼續觀賞吧，此劇與邪惡相
　　關，但這又如何？陛下和吾等無愧於心，必不受本劇影響。

（第一演員上。）

第一演員：狠毒心腸、手下無情、致命毒藥且無人知曉！太完
　　美了！

（他將毒藥灌進戲中國王之耳。）

哈姆雷特：他因貪財，在花園中將他毒死。本劇以流利義大利
　　文撰寫，之後諸位會見到兇手如何贏得貢札古夫人的芳心。

（國王起立。）

歐菲莉亞：國王起立了。

哈姆雷特：為什麼？有什麼事讓他受到驚嚇嗎？

皇后（對國王說）：怎麼了，陛下？

波隆尼爾：停止演出。

國王：點燈，我們走吧！

全體：燈光，點火，點燈！

（除哈姆雷特和赫瑞修，全體下。）

哈姆雷特：赫瑞修，你有觀察他嗎？

赫瑞修：非常仔細，殿下。

哈姆雷特：在演到下毒那段嗎？

赫瑞修：我非常仔細地觀察他。

哈姆雷特：啊哈！

（羅生克蘭和蓋登思鄧上。）

蓋登思鄧：殿下，是否能容我說幾句話？

哈姆雷特：閣下，你可以長篇大論。

蓋登思鄧：殿下，國王十分生氣。

哈姆雷特：他喝多了嗎，閣下？

蓋登思鄧：不，殿下，但他看起來很不舒服。皇后，也就是令堂
要我前來。她要我告訴您，她對您的行為感到驚訝與詫異。

哈姆雷特：喔，是什麼樣的兒子能讓母親感到如此驚訝，她還
有說別的嗎？

羅生克蘭：她希望您在就寢前，去她寢室談談。

哈姆雷特：好的，退下吧，吾友。（羅生克蘭、蓋登思鄧和赫瑞修
下。）夜晚此時是妖魔當道的時刻，鬼怪出世四處橫行，我
現在得以飲熱血並做白天見不得人的痛苦差事。現在我得
去找我母親——喔，我的心，千萬別改變心意，讓我對她殘
酷，卻不可失去分寸，我只用話語讓她心如刀割，但絕不出
手傷她，畢竟，她是我母親，而我是她兒子。

（哈姆雷特下。）

（國王、羅生克蘭和蓋登思鄧進入城堡一室。）

國王：我不喜歡他，我不願於他瘋癲時與其為伍，因此請準備同他前往英格蘭。

蓋登思鄧：遵命，陛下。吾等的神聖任務即是保守您的安全，因為眾人皆仰賴於您。

國王：請為此倉促之行預備，我們將用鏈鎖拴住目前四處遊蕩的恐懼。

（羅生克蘭和蓋登思鄧下，波隆尼爾上。）

波隆尼爾：他正在前往他母親的寢室，我將躲藏於簾幕之後側耳偷聽，相信她將能了解問題原委。我將在您就寢前拜會您，向您稟報所知一切。

國王：有勞你了，愛卿。（波隆尼爾下。）喔，我所犯下之罪甚為惡劣，所行已傳至上天。一如聖經中的該隱，我謀殺了胞兄！我不能禱告，即便我心甚想。我強烈的愧疚感壓倒強烈的慾望。我站在這像是一位有兩事待做之人，不曉得該先做何樣而同時將兩者忽略。這沾滿兄弟鮮血的受詛之手實在汙穢，難道天降甘霖還不足以將其洗刷雪白？我該如何祈禱？「乞求原諒我的殘忍謀殺」？罷了，畢竟我仍擁有謀殺所得之利：我的冠冕、雄心和皇后。罪人能被赦免且仍享罪行所帶來之利嗎？在這邪惡的世界，金錢能換得正義，通常也能買通律法，但在天堂則不然，那裡沒有詭計詐術。我該如何？若人無法懺悔罪孽該何去何從？喔，這景況是如此悽慘！喔，我靈魂如死般汙穢！躬身吧，頑固之膝！如鋼鐵般堅硬之心，像初生嬰兒肌膚般柔軟吧！願一切安然無事。

（國王跪下，哈姆雷特上。）

哈姆雷特（竊語）：現在下手輕而易
　　舉。（他拔劍。）但，不！若我現
　　在下手，他將上天堂。他是謀
　　殺我父親的惡人，而我這獨生
　　子卻為此送這惡人入天堂。喔，
　　這是愚昧之行，不是報仇！他趁
　　我父不意時下毒手，讓他來不及悔
　　過，罪行慾望如五月春花般盛放，
唯有上天知其功過。不，收回吧，寶劍，請為未來而預備。
當他酩酊大醉、狂暴盛怒、於床上行淫、賭博、咒罵，或做其
他違天之事時再對他下手，讓他腳跟往天堂踢，靈卻往地
獄栽，那才是他專屬之處。

（哈姆雷特下，國王起身。）

國王：我的言語傳達天際，但思緒仍留於世上，沒有思想的空
　　話將永遠上不了天堂。

（國王下。）

● **第四場**──────────────── P. 073

（皇后和波隆尼爾進入皇后寢室。）

波隆尼爾：他正往此處前來，請您語帶堅定，告訴他其惡作劇
　　已失控，而您已隱而不責多時，現在卻忍無可忍。我將安靜
　　地藏在此處。

哈姆雷特（從後台）：母后，母后！

165

皇后：快躲好，我聽見他的腳步聲了。

（波隆尼爾躲進布簾後，哈姆雷特上。）

哈姆雷特：母后，是什麼事呢？

皇后（意指克勞地國王）：哈姆雷特，你冒犯到父王了。

哈姆雷特（意指去世的哈姆雷特國王）：母親，您才冒犯了父王。

皇后：來吧，來吧，你用胡言亂語回答我。

哈姆雷特：去吧，去吧，您用惡毒之語責問我！

皇后：你忘了我的身分嗎？

哈姆雷特：當然沒有，您是皇后，是您丈夫的弟媳，而且——
　　我真不情願如此——您也是我母親。

皇后：不准如此對我說話。

哈姆雷特：來吧，請坐，別動。請在此處稍坐直到我將鏡子架
　　好，讓你照一照您的內心。

皇后：你想怎麼做？謀殺我嗎？救命，救命！

波隆尼爾（從簾幕後方）：救命！

哈姆雷特（拔劍）：此為何物──老鼠嗎？（他一劍刺穿布簾。）

波隆尼爾：喔，我命休矣！（波隆尼爾死。）

皇后：喔，天啊，你幹了什麼好事？

哈姆雷特：我不知道，那是國王嗎？

（哈姆雷特將波隆尼爾揪出來。）

皇后：喔，此舉真是魯莽又慘忍啊！

哈姆雷特：又有何差別呢，母后，此舉與謀殺國王和下嫁其弟
一樣卑鄙啊。

皇后：謀殺國王？

哈姆雷特：是啊，母后，我剛就是這麼說的。（對波隆尼爾：）你
這邪惡混蛋，再會了！我把你認成是國王，你現在終於了解
好管閒事的危險。（對皇后：）別再攤手了，坐下，我讓您更揪
心吧，除非您的心已化成鐵石心腸。

皇后：我究竟做了何事，讓你膽敢用這般無禮的字眼斥罵？

哈姆雷特：您的行為將純真之愛化作惡疾，讓婚禮誓言有如
賭徒之誓，令上天厭惡至極。

皇后：什麼行為？你究竟意指何事？

哈姆雷特：想想您前任丈夫，其人之善有如天神。現在看看你
現任丈夫，你難道有眼無珠嗎？你不能稱此為愛情，因在你
這般年紀不再有激情。有誰會在嫁給我父親後，再度嫁給
其弟？究竟是何種邪魔引誘您如此行事？喔，真令人可恥！
你怎能不因此感到羞愧？

皇后：喔，哈姆雷特，莫再説了。你已讓我雙目看透我的靈魂深處，令我見到永遠無法洗清的汙穢和汙點，我求你，別再説了！這些字眼就像利箭刺耳，別説了，親愛的哈姆雷特。

哈姆雷特：他是謀殺犯且是惡人，跟你前夫比起來天差地遠，他是將王為占為己有的畜牲。

皇后：別説了！

哈姆雷特：他只是位身披破布的國王！（鬼魂上，只有哈姆雷特看的見。）天使們，拯救我並在我身上看顧我吧！（對鬼魂説：）怎麼了，陛下？

皇后：喔，不，他瘋了！

哈姆雷特：您是前來責備您那仍未替您復仇的兒子嗎？告訴我吧！

鬼魂：別忘了，此次造訪是為了激勵你。但看看你的母親，她正在受苦，安撫她和她驚惶的靈魂吧，跟她談談吧，哈姆雷特。

哈姆雷特：母后，您還好嗎？

皇后：不好，你呢？你看著空中並對著虛空談話？你在看什麼呢？

哈姆雷特：看他，看「他」！看他是多麼蒼白！

皇后：親愛的兒子，那裡什麼也沒有啊。

哈姆雷特：您難道什麼都沒看到嗎？

皇后：什麼都沒有。

哈姆雷特：您什麼也都沒聽見嗎？

皇后：沒有，只有我們。

哈姆雷特：怎麼會，看那邊！看他正要離開了，我的父親，身著他在世的服裝，看啊——他要走出門了！

（鬼魂下。）

皇后：你能看見並不存在的事物。

哈姆雷特：母后，向神懺悔您的罪吧，懺悔過去所犯的罪惡，並避免將來之報應。

皇后：我兒，你已將我的心剖成兩半。

哈姆雷特：那麼，拋棄邪惡的那半，並用另一半更貞節地過活。晚安，但別上我叔父的床，即使你並非如此，也要假裝美德。你於今晚迴避此事，明日要迴避就更加容易，此後亦然。（指向波隆尼爾：）我為此事感到遺憾，但此為上天對我的懲罰，讓我因此事受苦，我將因置他死地而得到報應。再次晚安了，我得殘忍才能行善，這是壞事之始，而更糟的即將來臨，但母后，還有一件事……

皇后：是什麼呢？

哈姆雷特：我得前往英格蘭，您曉得嗎？

皇后：我已忘記此事，但，沒錯，你說的對。

哈姆雷特：我的兩位昔日同窗——我信任他們如我信任毒蛇——會與我同行，我們將一同遞送這封國王密信。就這樣吧，看人落入自己設的圈套

是件樂事，我已擬定計劃，他們將無法得逞。（**指向波隆尼爾：**）我要把屍體拖走，沒錯，這位朝臣在世時是位老奸人，現在卻如此僵硬沉默。晚安了，母后。

（**全體下，哈姆雷特將波隆尼爾拖走。**）

第四幕

●第一場 ─────────────────── P. 081

（**國王進入城堡一室與皇后在一起，皇后發出悲嘆。**）

國王：這悲嘆聲必定事出有因。

皇后：喔，我今晚看見駭人的景象！

國王：怎麼了，葛簇特？哈姆雷特是否安好？

皇后：如暴雨狂風般發狂，他聽見幕簾後傳出聲響，大喊：『老鼠』，然後一劍刺死波隆尼爾！

國王：喔，真是嚴重的罪行！若當時我在場，這將是我的下場。我們該如何解釋這血腥的作為？人民會責怪我們的，他在哪？

皇后：他已將屍首移走了。

國王：喔，葛簇特，我們得找到他，盡速送他上船，並想辦法解釋此惡行。（**羅生克蘭和蓋登思鄧上。**）兩位好，我們需要協助。哈姆雷特在瘋癲中殺死波隆尼爾，並將其屍首

拖走，去找他吧，並將屍首帶來教堂。求求兩位，動作快！
（羅生克蘭和蓋登思鄧下。）葛簇特，我們得與睿智的朋友們
商談，讓他們知道事情原委和解決之道，也許他們到時就
不會責怪我們。喔，走吧！我的靈魂充滿痛苦與哀傷。

（國王和皇后下。）

●第二場 P. 083

（哈姆雷特進入城堡另一室。）

哈姆雷特：屍首已藏好。

羅生克蘭和蓋登思鄧（從後台）：哈姆雷特！哈姆雷特殿下！

哈姆雷特：是誰在呼叫我？他們來了。

（羅生克蘭和蓋登思鄧上。）

羅生克蘭：殿下，屍體在何處呢？

哈姆雷特：我已將其與塵土和在一塊。

羅生克蘭：告訴我們地點吧，我們要將它帶到教堂。

哈姆雷特：為何你這海綿要如此質問我？

羅生克蘭：您當我是塊海綿？

哈姆雷特：是啊，一塊聽命於國王並吸收獎賞的海綿，當他要
　　從你那聽取情報時，只需擠壓你即可，然後你又變成一只
　　乾枯的綿塊。

羅生克蘭：我不懂您的意思，殿下。

哈姆雷特：這並不讓我感到吃驚，一段精彩的講演在愚人的
　　耳裡也是枉然，帶我去見國王吧。

（全體下。）

（國王與侍從進入城堡另一室。）

國王：我已派遣他們去尋找哈姆雷特和屍首。哈姆雷特是位危險人物！但我們不能讓其受到法律制裁，他深受人民喜愛，為了不掀波瀾，他的突然離去一定要看似是預先安排好的計劃。（羅生克蘭、蓋登思鄧和哈姆雷特上。）哈姆雷特，波隆尼爾呢？

哈姆雷特：正在吃晚餐呢。

國王：在吃晚餐！在何方？

哈姆雷特：不是在哪用餐，而是蟲子在哪吃他。

國王：好了，別這樣，告訴我們波隆尼爾身在何處？

哈姆雷特：在天堂，派人去那裡找他吧。若您的差使在那裡尋不見他的蹤影，您就自己去別處找他吧。倘若您在這個月內四處遍尋不著，那您走進大廳時將會聞到他的味道。

國王（對侍從說）：去那裡找他吧。

哈姆雷特：他將在那恭候各位。

（侍從下。）

國王：哈姆雷特，為了你自身的安危，我們得火速將你送走，快去準備吧。船已備好且風向正順，你得動身去英格蘭了。

哈姆雷特：好的，再會了，親愛的母親。

國王：我是深愛你的「父親」，哈姆雷特。

哈姆雷特：您是我的母親，父親與母親是丈夫與妻子，丈夫與妻子本是一體，因此您是我母親。現在，前往英格蘭吧！

（哈姆雷特下。）

國王（對羅生克蘭和蓋登思鄧說）：跟隨他吧，催促他，別延宕，我要他今晚就離開！遠走高飛！一切皆已備妥，快點吧！（除了國王全體下。）英格蘭國王，若您看重我的良善立意，您將照做我在信中要求的事。我要哈姆雷特立刻被處死，他像疾病般在我的血液中肆虐，讓我渾身不對勁，而您得醫治我的不適！在我確定事成之前，無論我運氣如何，我將無法快樂。

（國王下。）

●第四場 ——————————————— P. 088

（福丁布拉上，帶領軍隊在丹麥一處平原行軍。）

小福丁布拉（對營長說）：去向丹麥王行禮，詢問他是否仍然允許我軍於前往波蘭的途中，跨越其國土。

營長：是的，殿下。

（除了營長，全體下。哈姆雷特、羅生克蘭和蓋登思鄧上。）

哈姆雷特：您好，那是誰的軍隊呢？是由誰統帥，且來此何意？

營長：此為挪威大軍，殿下，由小福丁布拉統帥，是挪威王之姪，他正往波蘭去，欲爭奪其部分領土，希望能奪得一小部分價值不高的領土。

哈姆雷特：為何要如此做，波蘭王甚至不會派兵抵禦。

營長：剛好相反，殿下，波蘭大軍已在該地駐軍。

哈姆雷特：多麼浪費軍力啊！成千上萬的人將白白送死。謝謝您。

營長：願神與您同在，殿下。

（營長下。）

羅生克蘭：您準備好要動身了嗎，殿下？

哈姆雷特：我馬上來，你先去吧。（除了哈姆雷特，全體下。）這一切皆催促我報仇！若一人只會飲食酣睡，他算什麼呢？與野獸無異。使人理性思考的創造主必定希望我類善用此種能力。也許是我多慮，也許我只有一分智慧和三分膽怯，我不懂為何我總要等到擁有理由、意志、力量與方法時，才會說：『我必行此事』。他人的榜樣敦促我，看那由稚嫩的王子率領之大軍，他們願意為任何事獻上性命，就算是為了空殼也如此。至少小福丁布拉是為了替父親報仇而行動。那我呢？我父親被謀害，母親被玷汙，見到這往死裡去的兩萬大軍令我慚愧，他們願意為連蓋墓地都不夠大的彈丸之地而戰。喔，從今而後，但願我所有的念頭只有報仇一事。

（哈姆雷特下。）

●第五場 ————————————————— P. 091

（皇后和赫瑞修進入一室。）

皇后：歐菲莉亞想要什麼呢？

赫瑞修：她談到她父親，且胡言亂語。

皇后：讓她進來吧。（赫瑞修下。）我憂傷的心，一切好似是危險即將來臨之兆，愧疚使我充滿恐懼，越恐懼就越使人吐露不欲吐露之事。

（赫瑞修再上，歐菲莉亞上。）

歐菲莉亞：美麗的皇后在何方？

皇后：歐菲莉亞，你好嗎？

歐菲莉亞（唱歌）：他已命喪九泉，夫人，命喪九泉。他的頭顱長草，腳下生石。

皇后：但歐菲莉亞……

（國王上。）

歐菲莉亞：聽啊：（唱歌）「他的斂衣如高山雪白，他躺臥在甜美的白花叢中，被我們的淚水澆灌。」

國王：你好嗎，美麗的女孩？

皇后：她太想念她父親了。

歐菲莉亞（唱歌）：「明日是情人節，朝晨之時，我這少女將駐足你窗前，成為你的情人。他將起身，穿上衣裳，敞開臥室之門，讓女子進門並停留片刻，隨後純潔不再。她說：『在你讓我進門之前，你承諾過娶我為妻。』他說：『此話沒錯，倘若你沒上我的床。』」

國王：她這樣已多久了？

歐菲莉亞：但願一切平安，但我止不住淚，特別是想到他們將他葬入冰冷之地！我兄長得知此消息，多謝各位的忠告佳言。來吧，我的座車！晚安了，諸位親愛的夫人。晚安，夫人們。晚安，晚安！

（歐菲莉亞下。）

國王（對赫瑞修說）：跟隨她，好嗎？（赫瑞修下。）喔，這是哀慟過甚之毒，出自她父親之死。喔，葛簇特，當悲傷襲來，並非一絲一縷，而是如大軍湧入！先是她父親被殺，接著你兒子離去，人們對波隆尼爾去世之說感到憤怒，他們認為我與此事有關。可憐的歐菲莉亞！思緒崩亂。雷爾提已悄悄從法國返回，他已知悉他父親死因之謠。（他聽見台下傳來的聲響。）那是什麼？我的侍從呢？

175

（一位男子上。）

男子：陛下，快逃命！雷爾提率領一群暴徒已擊垮您的士兵，暴民們稱他為「王」，他們呼喊著：『我們已做出選擇！我們要雷爾提為王！』

（台下傳出聲響。）

國王：大門被擊破了！

（雷爾提上，身後有幾名丹麥人，男子下。）

雷爾提：國王在哪？（對隨從：）看守大門。

丹麥人們：是的，遵命。

（丹麥人下。）

雷爾提（對國王）：喔，你這邪惡國王，把我父的命還來！

皇后：冷靜，親愛的雷爾提。

雷爾提：一丁點冷靜都是對吾父的背叛。

國王：你為何如此憤怒？告訴我！

雷爾提：我父親在哪？

國王：去世了。

雷爾提：我將為我父親報仇！

國王：親愛的雷爾提，為了報仇，你願意殺害朋友和仇敵嗎？

雷爾提：我父親的敵人將一律受死。

國王：你想知道仇人是誰嗎？

雷爾提：當然。

國王：我與令尊之死無關，我為此感到悲傷。

丹麥人們（從台下）：讓她進來。

雷爾提：那是什麼聲音？（**歐菲莉亞再上，她的衣服與頭髮上插著稻草與花朵。**）歐菲莉亞！喔，熱氣烤乾我腦！鹹淚水灼傷我眼！奉天之名，我將為你的瘋癲報仇！親愛的女孩，心腸好的妹妹，甜美的歐菲莉亞！喔，老天！一位年輕女子的智慧怎能如老人般垂死？

歐菲莉亞（唱歌）：「那兒，在他墳上……嘿噥噥呢，嘿噥呢……我們所流之淚……」

雷爾提：若你仍保有理智，也不能如現在這般激發我的復仇的心志。

歐菲莉亞（唱歌）：「他是否會再來？不，不，他已赴黃泉，去了你的臨終之榻，永無再來之日，他的鬍鬚白如雪，他走了，他走了，我們只能悲嘆，願神憐憫他的靈魂。」（**歐菲莉亞下。**）

國王：雷爾提，我深感同悲，去找你睿智的朋友，他們將傾聽你我之言並作出決斷。若他們判我有罪，那麼你將接掌我的國王、王位、生命和我所擁有的一切。若情況並非如此，請保持耐心，我們將設法彌補你的損失。

雷爾提：就這樣吧，他死得不明不白又秘密下葬，沒有貴族應有的正式儀式，這全都亟需解釋。

國王：而你將會得到解答，有罪之人，斧必落之，現在，同我離開吧。

（全體下。）

●第六場 P. 098

（赫瑞修與一僕從進入另一室。）

赫瑞修：是誰欲找我談話？

僕從：是水手們，閣下，他們要有信要交給你。

赫瑞修：讓他們進來吧。

（僕從下，水手們上。）

第一水手：您好，閣下。這封信是前往英格蘭的大使捎來的。

赫瑞修（閱讀）：「親愛的赫瑞修，當你讀完此信後，請安排這幾位水手晉見陛下，他們也有捎信給他。我們啟程兩日後遇上海盜，在緊接而來的戰鬥中，我登上他們的船艦，當他們離開我方船隻後，我一人則成為他們的俘虜。他們善待我，希望也有所回報。讓陛下收下我捎去的信函，然後如逃離死劫般地飛速來找我，我有讓你瞠目結舌的話要跟你說，

不便寫在信裡。這些善良的傢伙會將你帶到我這。羅生克蘭和蓋登思鄧仍在前往英格蘭的途中,我有許多關於他們的事要告訴你。哈姆雷特敬上。」（對水手說：）與我一同去晉見陛下吧,之後再帶我去找哈姆雷特。

（全體下。）

●第七場 ——————————————P. 100

（國王和雷爾提進入城堡中另一室。）

國王：現在你已知此事全貌,哈姆雷特在殺了令尊後,試圖要殺我。

雷爾提：看來此事為真,但請告訴我,您為何沒因這些罪行而懲罰他？

國王：是基於兩項特別的原因。皇后,他的母親,幾乎是為哈姆雷特而活,而我愛她太深,不願讓她傷心。同時,百姓也愛戴他,無論我所言為何,他們皆不願相信,民怨將對我不利。

雷爾提（悲憤貌）：我就這麼失去一位高貴的父親,而我小妹被逼得發瘋,我一定會復仇。

國王：別因此失眠,切勿認為我已忘卻這些過往之事,你不久將會得知下文。我愛令尊,我也愛自己,我將會為哈姆雷特的罪行報仇。

（信使上。）

信使：有信函,陛下,是哈姆雷特捎來的。這封是給您的,這封是給皇后的。

國王：哈姆雷特捎來的信！是誰將信送來的？

信使：是水手們，陛下。

（信使下。）

國王：雷爾提，你得聽聽這信。（閱讀：）「陛下，我已回國，明日我想見您，並告訴您我突然且奇異的返回之因。哈姆雷特。」這是什麼意思？其他人也一併返回了嗎？

雷爾提：這是哈姆雷特的筆跡嗎？

國王：是啊，這究竟是何意？

雷爾提：我不曉得，陛下。但讓他來吧，這溫暖我的痛苦心靈，因我將得以迅速復仇。

國王：雷爾提，你願意聽我的建言嗎？

雷爾提：願意，陛下——只要您不建議我留哈姆雷特活口。

國王：我有個將他置於死地的計劃，就連他母親也會認為那是意外。

雷爾提：陛下，我願意親手一試。

國王：聽說你擅長擊劍，在競技場上極為出眾。其實哈姆雷特很忌妒你的名聲，並亟欲打敗你。讓我問你一個問題，你最想如何對哈姆雷特下手，以展現你欲為父復仇之決心？

雷爾提：在教堂中割斷他的咽喉！

國王：無論何處皆可復仇，但，好雷爾提，這是更好的計劃：哈姆雷特將獲悉你在此處，我們將派遣眾人頌讚你的擊劍技巧，並打賭誰將在決鬥中得勝——你或哈姆雷特。毫不知情的他，將不會檢查劍尖，你可以輕易挑選一把劍尖沒有保護套的劍，接著在一陣比劃後，你將能為父親報一劍之仇。

雷爾提：就這麼做吧！為確保此事成功，我將在劍尖塗上毒藥，我已取得此毒，其效力之強，沒有解藥可解。

國王：讓我們再思考一番，若計劃失敗，將讓我們顏面掃地，與其計劃失敗不如作罷，因此我們得擬定備案。讓我想想……啊！我想到了！當你倆決鬥時，你們將口乾舌燥，當他要求飲水時，我將為他預備一杯水，若他恰好躲過你的毒劍，他也將飲毒而亡。

（皇后上，悲慟欲絕。）

皇后：悲慘之事接踵而至──令妹溺水身亡了，雷爾提。

雷爾提：溺水！喔，在何處？

皇后：在小溪旁有一棵柳樹，其枝葉倒映在清澈的溪水上。當令妹在該地編織花環時，她爬上伸至溪上的枝幹想將花環掛上，但枝幹卻應聲而斷，她跌入那嗚咽的溪水。有那麼一會兒，她的衣服散開並將她托浮至水面有如人魚，但接著湍急溪流湧上，她的衣物將這可憐人拖進泥濘而亡。

雷爾提：可憐啊，然後她就溺斃了？

皇后：溺斃了，溺斃了……

雷爾提：你已飲下太多水，可憐的歐菲莉亞，我將努力止住淚水，但我只是凡夫俗子，我沒辦法。（他哭泣。）當淚水流乾後，我內心將不再有任何感情。（雷爾提下。）

國王：讓我們跟他去吧，葛簇特，我已盡我所能以平息他的憤怒！現在這件悲傷之事又再度令他發怒，因此，讓我們跟他走吧。

（國王和皇后下。）

第五幕

●第一場

（掘墓人和其幫手進入教堂墓地。）

掘墓人：即使她自殺身亡，也將舉辦基督教葬禮？

幫手：我是這麼聽說的。

掘墓人：怎麼會呢？難道她是因自衛而溺水身亡？

幫手：驗屍官說她並非自殺身亡，人們願意如此相信，是因為她生前是位善良的姑娘。

掘墓人：誰知道？又有誰在意？我只想大飲一場，你何不去酒館幫我倆買些酒？

（幫手下，哈姆雷特和赫瑞修上，站在遠處，看著掘墓人挖墳並唱歌。）

哈姆雷特：他怎會對此工作如此冷血？怎能邊唱歌邊掘墓呢？

赫瑞修：他已習以為常，以至於他不會對此事多做思考。

哈姆雷特：你這樣說應該沒錯，只有不辛勤工作的人才有時間胡思亂想。

掘墓人（唱歌）：「鋤啊鋤，鏟啊鏟，挖個深洞給新訪客。給美麗姑娘一席裹屍衣，她馬上將在此地長眠。」

（他的鏟子碰到一個骷髏頭，並將其拋到地面。）

哈姆雷特：那是一個骷髏頭，這會是律師的頭骨嗎？他的辯詞、案件、證據和招數都在哪呢？他為何放任這魯莽之人用髒鏟擺弄他的屍骨？他不是該譴責如此嚴重的侵犯？嗯……這傢伙也有可能是位有錢的地主，卻落此田地，任土泥混進腦袋裡？他所有的地契與法律文件只能放在這只棺材裡，難道這位地主不能擁有比此更多的安葬空間嗎？

赫瑞修：殿下，多一吋都不行。

哈姆雷特：我要跟這傢伙談談。（**對掘墓人說：**）這是誰的墓呢？

掘墓人：閣下，是我的。

哈姆雷特：我是說，你是在替哪位先生掘墓呢？

掘墓人：不是為先生掘墓，閣下。

哈姆雷特：那是為哪位女士呢？

掘墓人：也不是為女士掘墓，閣下。

哈姆雷特：是誰將葬在此地呢？

掘墓人：一位生前是小姐的亡者，閣下。但願她靈魂安息，她已去世了。

哈姆雷特：你遣詞用字真是小心啊！你當掘墓人多久了呢？

掘墓人：我從三十年前，哈姆雷特國王打敗老福丁布拉的那天開始掘墓。那天正是小哈姆雷特誕生的日子，他現在已被遣送至英格蘭了。

哈姆雷特：他為什麼被遣送到英格蘭呢？

掘墓人：因為他發瘋了，他得在那恢復理智，倘若他無法的話，也無妨。

哈姆雷特：為什麼？

掘墓人：不會有英格蘭人發現的，那裡的人都跟他一樣瘋癲。

哈姆雷特：請問，被埋葬之人要多久才會腐化呢？

掘墓人：八或九年。（**他拾起骷髏頭。**）這是一個骷髏頭，這個骷髏頭已被埋葬二十三年了。

哈姆雷特：那是誰的頭骨呢？

掘墓人：閣下，這是約利克的頭骨，他是國王的弄臣。

哈姆雷特：讓我看看。（他拿著骷髏頭。）唉，可憐的約利克！我認識他，赫瑞修。他生前是位給人帶來無限樂趣的傢伙，我小時候他至少背著我一千次，現在想起來真令人傷感！那些玩笑、把戲、歌曲和歡樂時光都去哪了？有誰能再嘲笑你的露齒笑容？現在就去我愛人的閨房吧，告訴她，不管她畫上多厚的妝，都終將化為骷髏，讓她笑笑吧。赫瑞修，你認為亞歷山大大帝埋在土裡時也是這副德性嗎？

赫瑞修：一模一樣。

哈姆雷特：聞起來也是這樣嗎？我呸！（丟下骷髏頭。）

赫瑞修：殿下，也是一模一樣。

哈姆雷特：我們的軀體終將成為如此卑賤的東西啊，赫瑞修！就連亞歷山大高貴的遺骸，都可能成為堵住洞口的塞子。

赫瑞修：您太多慮了，哈姆雷特。

哈姆雷特：你這樣思考片刻吧：亞歷山大去世，亞歷山大被埋葬，亞歷山大變成遺骸，而遺骸就是塵土。我們用塵土來做陶土，而這塊陶土某天可能就會成為啤酒桶的塞子。凱薩大帝去世後成為陶土，又成為防漏氣的塞子。喔，這位舉世敬佩的偉人竟可能成為防止漏風的補牆黏土！但，我說夠了，你看，國王來了。（*神父上，領著一列隊伍。國王、皇后、雷爾提和悼念者跟隨其後。侍從抬著一具棺材。*）棺材裡究竟是誰呢？皇后來了，但悼念者甚少，意味這是自殺，一定是貴族之輩，我們躲起來看吧。

（*哈姆雷特和赫瑞修躲起來。*）

雷爾提：還有什麼其他的儀式？

第一神父：我們已盡力為她的喪禮而努力了，她的死因令人存疑，應該要被埋葬在不被祝福的墓地，並在其上投擲卵石。然而她卻得以在此進行儀式，用花朵、禱告和喪鐘送別其處女之身。

雷爾提（*悲傷*）：僅此而已嗎？

第一神父：僅此而已。我們若用對待善終亡者的儀式待她，便褻瀆了喪禮。

雷爾提：讓她入土為安吧，讓紫羅蘭從她美麗純潔的玉體綻放！你這位自私的神父，當你在地獄哀嚎時，舍妹將成為天使。

哈姆雷特：什麼——那是美麗的歐菲莉亞？

皇后（*撒花*）：甜美的鮮花應歸於甜美的姑娘，再會了。我原本希望你能嫁給哈姆雷特。親愛的，我想將花朵撒在你的新娘床上，但是，我卻只能撒在你的墳上。

雷爾提：喔，願無數災禍降臨在使她發狂的人身上！在我再次將她擁入懷中之前，別埋葬她！（*他跳進墳墓。*）現在把土撒在我倆身上吧！

哈姆雷特（*上前*）：此為何人？是誰讓他如此悲戚？

雷爾提：這位不速之客又是誰？

哈姆雷特（跳進墳墓）：是我，丹麥王子哈姆雷特。

雷爾提（與其大打出手）：她的死全都是因你造成的，你這畜生！

哈姆雷特：你錯了，請將手從我脖子上拿開。

國王（對侍從）：把他們拉開！

皇后：哈姆雷特！哈姆雷特！

（侍從將他們分開，他們出了墳墓。）

哈姆雷特：我將與他戰鬥到嚥下最後一口氣！

皇后：喔，吾兒，所為何事呢？

哈姆雷特：我愛歐菲莉亞！就算四萬個兄弟的愛都不及我對她的愛。

國王：喔，他瘋了，雷爾提！

皇后：看在神的份上，別煩他！

哈姆雷特（對雷爾提）：你是來哀哭的嗎？跳入她的墳墓以展現你對她的愛？若你想陪葬，我也願意。若你想大吼大叫發洩怒火，我也會同你這麼做。

皇后：這太瘋狂了。

哈姆雷特：雷爾提，你為何要歸咎於我呢？我總是如敬重親兄弟般敬重你，但這不打緊，請你依意志行事吧，人性難改，情緒難平。

（哈姆雷特下。）

國王：親愛的赫瑞修，照顧好他。（赫瑞修下。）（對雷爾提：）耐心點，想想我們昨晚所談論的事吧。你將會有其他的出手機會。

（全體下。）

（哈姆雷特和赫瑞修進入城堡的一間大廳。）

哈姆雷特：在我信中，我提到我有事要親口告訴你。我們三人前往英格蘭——羅生克蘭、蓋登思鄧和我。我心中老是惴惴不安，令我難以安眠。衝動的念頭突然竄出，也感謝老天讓我如此衝動，我披上水手的外套，在黑暗中摸黑去找他們。在我終於尋見他們後，他們正在沉睡，我偷走他們攜帶的信函。回到寢室後，我不顧禮數，打開這些信函，便發現——喔，多可怕的皇家密謀啊！——那是我們國王寫給英格蘭王的信，上面寫著，只要一打開這封信，連磨利斧頭的時間都不需要，請立刻砍下我的首級！

赫瑞修（震驚）：真的嗎？

哈姆雷特：這就是那封信——你自己讀吧。但你可想知道我接下來的所作所為？

赫瑞修：您請說吧。

哈姆雷特：我坐下來撰寫一封新信，在信中，我提到英格蘭王和丹麥王一向交情甚篤，我寫，看在兩人的情誼上，此事不須爭論，他得立即處死捎信來的信使們。他們將不得進行臨終懺悔，而我當然以我母后丈夫的名義署名。我行囊中有我父王的玉璽戒指，它與目前國王的玉璽相吻合。我照之前那封信的折法把信折妥，用蠟緘信，並妥善地將它放置於第一封信的原位。羅生克蘭和蓋登思鄧將永遠不知道此調換之計，接著，隔日就是我們在海上交火的日子，我們被海盜攻擊。之後發生的事，你皆悉數了解。

赫瑞修：所以蓋登思鄧和羅生克蘭是直接赴死？

第五幕

第二場

187

哈姆雷特：怎麼了，他們非常熱愛他們的工作呀！我不因此感到愧疚，他們的命運是他們自己所造成的，當一位弱者闖入兩位武士的刀光劍影中，他們就得承受受傷的風險。

赫瑞修：我們的國王怎麼會如此？

哈姆雷特：他殺了我父王，毀掉母后的名譽，又阻止我登基，接著還想置我於死地！若我能親手了結他該有多好？

赫瑞修：當英格蘭王收到你的信後，我們國王將恍然大悟。

哈姆雷特：是的，但在此期間，我掌握先機。要取某人的性命不需耽誤太多時間，但我很抱歉，親愛的赫瑞修，我對雷爾提失控，我將想辦法彌補他，但他的悲傷也讓我更加悲痛。

赫瑞修：安靜，有人來了。

（奧斯利克上。）

奧斯利克：殿下，歡迎回到丹麥。

哈姆雷特：衷心感謝你，閣下。

奧斯利克：殿下，陛下要我告訴您，他十分看好您的劍術，也對此下了大注。如您所知，雷爾提也是位劍術精湛的劍士，聽說沒有人的劍術能超越他，而國王以六匹駿馬作為賭注，認為您能在決鬥中打敗雷爾提。賭注的詳細情況是這樣的：在十二回合的交戰中，雷爾提不能擊中您超過三次。另一方面，雷爾提說他將在十二回合中擊中您九次，若殿下願意接受挑戰，此賭注將立刻進行。

哈姆雷特：我願意，我將盡力為國王贏得勝利。倘若失敗，我也只是羞愧與受皮肉之傷罷了。

奧斯利克：殿下，我將轉告您的訊息。

（奧斯利克下。）

赫瑞修：殿下，你這局恐怕會賭輸。

哈姆雷特：我不同意，自從雷爾提前往法國後，我一直都在練習，我一定能贏得賭注。我並非毫不緊張，但這並不要緊。

赫瑞修（擔心貌）：若您對此有任何不祥之感，我會告訴他們您身體不適。

哈姆雷特：才不呢，我不相信惡兆或不祥之感，就連一隻麻雀之死也有其特別天命。若死亡欲迎面而來，它必不會拖延；若死亡不願他日再與我相逢，它必會立刻現身。不管如何，遲早要面臨死亡，準備好面對死亡實為要事。

（國王、皇后、雷爾提、貴族大臣、奧斯利克和侍從拿著寶劍上。）

國王：哈姆雷特，與雷爾提握手吧。（國王將雷爾提的手放在哈姆雷特手中。）

哈姆雷特（對雷爾提）：請原諒我，閣下。我有愧於你，你必定聽說我最近魂不守舍，若我之前冒犯你，請原諒我。

雷爾提：我接受你的道歉。

國王：把寶劍給他們吧，年輕的奧斯利克。哈姆雷特，你知道賭注為何嗎？

哈姆雷特：一清二楚，陛下，您將賭注下在較弱之人的身上。

國王：我可不這麼認為，我看過你倆的劍術，我相信你將讓雷爾提難以招架。

雷爾提（發現他仍未拿到毒劍）：這把劍太重了，讓我看看另一把劍。

哈姆雷特：這把很適合我。

（他們準備決戰，僕人帶了幾杯酒上。）

國王：將酒杯置於桌上，若哈姆雷特勝利，我將為他的康健乾杯。

（開始比賽，哈姆雷特率先得分。）

國王：我要為此乾杯，敬你的體能，哈姆雷特。（他喝了點酒，接著當號角響起時，他偷偷將毒藥置入另一杯酒中並舉杯給哈姆雷特喝。）喝一口吧，哈姆雷特。

哈姆雷特：我想先比賽，先暫且放著。（對雷爾提：）放手過來吧。

（他們接著比賽，哈姆雷特又得分。）

國王（對皇后說）：我們的兒子將贏得勝利。

皇后：但他體能不好且喘不過氣。（對哈姆雷特：）哈姆雷特，拿著我的手帕擦掉額頭的汗吧。（拿起國王擱置一旁要給哈姆雷特喝的毒酒。）乾杯，祝你好運，哈姆雷特。

國王：葛簇特，別喝！

皇后：陛下，若您不介意，我想喝。

（她喝了一口並把酒杯遞給哈姆雷特。）

國王（竊語）：那是毒酒！為時已晚了。

哈姆雷特（對皇后）：還沒，謝謝，我晚點再喝。

（他們繼續進行劍術比賽，在一陣激烈的搏鬥後，雷爾提用毒劍刺中哈姆雷特。比賽進行一半，兩人拋下實劍進行扭打，雙方皆疏忽而拾起對方的劍，接著哈姆雷特用毒劍刺傷了雷爾提，此時皇后倒下。）

赫瑞修：他們都在流血！（對哈姆雷特：）您還好嗎，殿下？

奧斯利克（對雷爾提）：你還好嗎，雷爾提？

雷爾提：沒想到飛鳥也會自投羅網，奧斯利克，我被自己的奸計所殺。

哈姆雷特：皇后還好嗎？

國王：她看見你流血而昏倒。

皇后：不，不！是酒，是酒！喔，我親愛的哈姆雷特！我被下毒了。

（皇后身亡。）

哈姆雷特：喔，太邪惡了！停止一切！深鎖大門！揪出叛賊！

（雷爾提倒下。）

雷爾提：叛賊就在此地，哈姆雷特。哈姆雷特，你死期已到。世上沒有解藥能救你，你只剩不到半小時可活，您手上握的那把邪惡之劍，其尖端並沒有護套，且已被下毒。我們皆被此劍而傷，我倒臥於此，再也無法站起，而您母親也被下毒，我已無可奉告。國王──這一切皆歸咎於國王。

哈姆雷特：劍尖被下毒？那麼毒藥啊，請發揮效用吧！

（哈姆雷特用劍刺了國王。）

奧斯利克和貴族大臣：叛國賊！叛國賊！

哈姆雷特：喝吧，你這奸人！隨我母后去吧！

（哈姆雷特逼國王喝下毒酒，國王身亡。）

雷爾提：他罪有應得，這都是他的詭計，我們原諒彼此吧，哈姆雷特。我原諒您造成我與我父親的死，也懇請您原諒我殺了你。（雷爾提身亡。）

哈姆雷特：願上天釋放你的靈魂，我將隨你而去。哀傷的皇后，永別了！我將撒手人間，赫瑞修，你還活著，向不知情的人訴說我的故事吧。

赫瑞修：別認為我將苟活，毒酒仍然有剩。

哈姆雷特：你是位正人君子，把酒杯給我吧，放手吧，看在上蒼之名，讓我喝吧。（哈姆雷特從赫瑞修手中接過酒杯。）喔，親愛的赫瑞修，若你曾視我為知己，這陣子先遠離享樂，在如此殘酷的塵世，用沉痛的口吻訴說我的故事。（聽見行軍及槍火聲。）那是什麼聲音呢？

奧斯利克：小福丁布拉王在波蘭取得勝利，正踏上歸途，而英格蘭派來的大使也捎來消息。

哈姆雷特：喔，我行將就木，赫瑞修！我將無法活著聽見從英格蘭捎來的消息，但我預言福丁布拉將成為丹麥的下任國王，他得到我臨終前的支持，務必告訴他——（*他未能將此話說盡，接下來一片靜默，哈姆雷特身亡。*）

赫瑞修：這是條高貴生命的逝去，晚安，親愛的王子，願天使高唱直到您安息！

（*福丁布拉、大使和其他人等入。*）

福丁布拉：這裡發生了什麼事？

赫瑞修：你們想看何種光景呢？若想看悲傷和悽愴的場面，就無需再搜尋了。

第一大使：此畫面令人備感淒涼，我們太晚從英格蘭捎來消息，下命令的人再也收不到回音，羅生克蘭和蓋登思鄧已死，我們要向誰討謝酬呢？

赫瑞修（*指著國王*）：就算他仍能說話，他也不會開口。他從未下令處死那兩人，我將對您據實以告所有詳情。

福丁布拉：立刻告訴我們吧，我在此國有繼承王位的權利，我現在將要求取得此權力。

赫瑞修：我也將談及這事，至於現在，我們先恭敬地處理亡者遺體吧。

福丁布拉：請四位軍官將哈姆雷特視為軍人，搬運他的遺體。至於他的喪禮，讓軍樂和軍禮大聲讚頌他。將所有的遺體高抬吧！這樣的場景只適合戰場，不適宜此地。去吧，吩咐士兵們開始射擊禮炮。

（*禮炮聲響，鼓聲齊下，遺體皆被搬走，全體下。*）

Literary Glossary ● 文學詞彙表

aside 竊語

一種台詞。演員在台上講此台詞時，其他角色是聽不見的。角色通常藉由竊語來向觀眾抒發內心感受。

- Although she appeared to be calm, the heroine's **aside** revealed her inner terror.
  雖然女主角看似冷靜，但她的**竊語**透露出她內在的恐懼。

backstage 後台

一個戲院空間。演員都在此處準備上台，舞台布景也存放此處。

- Before entering, the villain impatiently waited **backstage**.
  在上台前，壞人在**後台**焦躁地等待。

cast 演員；卡司陣容

戲劇的全體演出人員。

- The entire **cast** must attend tonight's dress rehearsal.
  全體演員必須參加今晚的正式排練。

character 角色

故事或戲劇中虛構的人物。

- Mighty Mouse is one of my favorite cartoon **characters**.
  太空飛鼠是我最愛的卡通**人物**之一。

climax 劇情高峰

戲劇或小說中主要衝突的結局。

- The outlaw's capture made an exciting **climax** to the story.
  逃犯落網成為故事中最刺激的**精彩情節**。

comedy 喜劇

有趣好笑的戲劇、電影和電視劇，並有快樂完美的結局。

- My friends and I always enjoy a Jim Carrey **comedy**.
  我朋友和我總是很喜歡金凱瑞演的**喜劇**。

conflict 戲劇衝突

故事主要的角色較量、勢力對抗或想法衝突。

- Dr. Jekyll and Mr. Hyde illustrates the **conflict** between good and evil.
  《變身怪醫》描述善惡之間的**衝突**。

conclusion 尾聲

解決情節衝突的方法，使故事結束。

- That play's **conclusion** was very satisfying. Every conflict was resolved. 該劇的**結局**十分令人滿意，所有的衝突都被圓滿解決。

dialogue 對白

小說或戲劇角色所說的話語。

- Amusing **dialogue** is an important element of most comedies.
  有趣的**對白**是大多喜劇中重要的元素之一。

drama 戲劇

故事，通常非喜劇類型，特別是寫來讓演員在戲劇或電影中演出。

- The TV **drama** about spies was very suspenseful.
  那齣關於間諜的電視**劇**非常懸疑。

event 事件

發生的事情；特別的事。

- The most exciting **event** in the story was the surprise ending.
  故事中最精彩的**事件**是意外的結局。

introduction 簡介

一篇簡短的文章，呈現並解釋小說或戲劇的劇情。

- The **introduction** to Frankenstein is in the form of a letter.
  《科學怪人》的**簡介**是以信件的型式呈現。

---

motive 動機

一股內在或外在的力量，迫使角色做出某些事情。

- What was that character's **motive** for telling a lie?
  那個角色說謊的**動機**為何？

---

passage 段落

書寫作品的部分內容，範圍短至一行，長至幾段。

- His favorite **passage** from the book described herman's childhood.
  他在書中最喜歡的**段落**描述了該漁夫的童年。

---

playwright 劇作家

戲劇的作者。

- William Shakespeare is the world's most famous **playwright**.
  威廉莎士比亞是世界上最知名的**劇作家**。

---

plot 情節

故事或戲劇中一連串的因果事件，導致最終結局。

- The **plot** of that mystery story is filled with action.
  該推理故事的**情節**充滿打鬥。

---

point of view 觀點

由角色的心理層面來看待故事發展的狀況。

- The father's **point of view** about elopement was quite different from the daughter's. 父親對於私奔的**看法**與女兒迥然不同。

prologue 序幕

在戲劇第一幕開始前的介紹。

- The **playwright** described the main characters in the **prologue** to the play.

  劇作家在**序幕**中描述了主要角色。

....

quotation 名句

被引述的文句；某角色所說的詞語；在引號內的文字。

- A popular **quotation** from Julius Caesar begins, "Friends, Romans, countrymen . . ."

  《凱薩大帝》中**常被引用的文句**開頭是：「各位朋友，各位羅馬人，各位同胞……」。

....

role 角色

演員在劇中揣摩表演的人物。

- Who would you like to see play the **role** of Romeo?

  你想看誰飾演羅密歐這個**角色**呢？

....

sequence 順序

故事或事件發生的時序。

- Sometimes actors rehearse their scenes out of **sequence**.

  演員有時會不按**順序**排練他們出場的戲。

....

setting 情節背景

故事發生的地點與時間。

- This play's **setting** is New York in the 1940s.

  戲劇的**背景設定**於 1940 年代的紐約。

soliloquy 獨白

角色向觀眾發表想法的一番言論，猶如自言自語。

■ One famous **soliloquy** is Hamlet' speech that begins, "To be, or not to be . . ."
哈姆雷特中最知名的**獨白**是：「生，抑或是死……」。

....

symbol 象徵

用以代表其他事物的人或物。

■ In Hawthorne's famous novel, the scarlet letter is a **symbol** for adultery.
在霍桑知名的小說中，紅字是姦淫罪的**象徵**。

....

theme 主題

戲劇或小說的主要意義；中心思想。

■ Ambition and revenge are common **themes** in Shakespeare's plays.
在莎士比亞的劇作中，雄心壯志與報復是常見的**主題**。

....

tragedy 悲劇

嚴肅且有悲傷結局的戲劇。

■ Macbeth, the shortest of Shakespeare's plays, is a **tragedy**.
莎士比亞最短的劇作《馬克白》是部**悲劇**。